SEASONS OF INTIMACY

SEASONS OF INTIMACY

A Story of Timing and Trust

When timing is everything, love waits—
through whispered moments, unspoken truths,
and a passion that deepens over time.

Jason Schubert

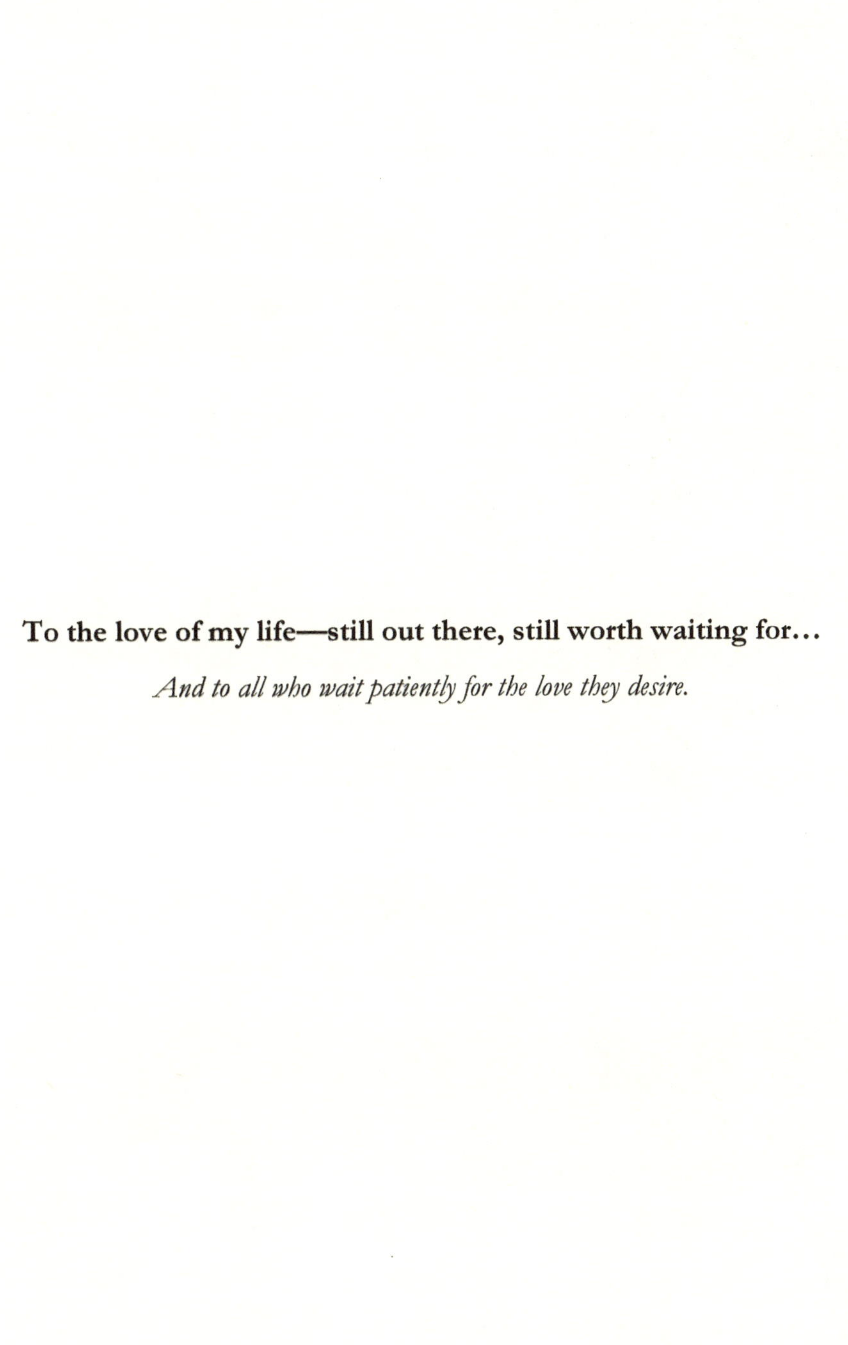

To the love of my life—still out there, still worth waiting for...

And to all who wait patiently for the love they desire.

Love isn't a fleeting spark,

*but a steady flame
that weathers time, distance, and fear*

When timing is everything,

*love waits patiently—
through whispered moments, unspoken truths,
and a passion that deepens over time*

A slow-burning love story,

*unfolding quietly
across the seasons*

WINTER

SNOWBOUND

Her eyes were already heavy from the drive, and now the darkness made it worse. Snowflakes attacked the windshield like a *Star Wars* hyperdrive scene, making it feel as if she were moving much faster than she was. The wipers struggled to keep up. No tire tracks and no other lights. She could barely even see the road anymore.

Her knuckles whitened around the steering wheel. While she was no stranger to harsh conditions, this area was unfamiliar, yet she knew better than to expect any signs of civilization soon. Her last surge of adrenaline had faded.

Then, a flicker of hope—lights ahead, clustered in the distance, just beginning to come into view. She slowed, refusing to let her excitement override caution. She exhaled in relief. An outdated neon sign glowed: *Vacancy*.

A few hundred feet away, inside the modest motel, a man leaned over the sink rinsing his hands while staring blankly into the mirror. He was grateful not to be hurt, and to the lone truck driver who pulled him from his car, which was now likely buried under several feet of snow a few miles away.

Whatever luck he had left, he knew his options were limited. Whatever came next would have to wait until the weather improved. He inhaled deeply, trying to relax for the first time since the accident. Tearing off a towel, he dried his hands, wiped his face, and tossed it in the bin. He was done with the unexpected. No more excitement for the night.

Walking in from the storm, she shook off the snow and began to peel off her coat. She rolled her eyes, gave an audible sigh, and offered the girl at the front desk a forced smile.

As she approached, the girl's expression looked reluctant, almost nervous. When she asked for a room, the girl hesitated.

"Um… well… we kind of have a room."

"Perfect. I'll take it!"

Before she could break the awkward silence, the man stepped out from the nearby bathroom.

The clerk froze, her brows furrowed as she realized the situation—whatever this was, it wasn't simple. He'd only told the clerk he wanted a room when he arrived, before quickly retreating to the bathroom. He hadn't officially checked in. With his coat folded over his arm, he apologized for interrupting and placed his identification on the counter, signaling he was now ready for his key.

The clerk glanced between the two of them, her discomfort growing with every passing second. She slowly closed her eyes and shook her head, a silent cue they both understood. The man avoided eye contact, but could feel the woman's glare. The clerk's discomfort was palpable. Finally, the young girl opened a drawer and placed the key to room #7 on the counter.

Knowing the man had arrived first, but hadn't checked in, the clerk turned to him as if expecting him to defer the room to the newly arrived guest.

Nothing.

Frustrated, the clerk muttered, "I seriously don't get paid enough for this," before walking off, leaving the key lying awkwardly between them.

He felt her gaze again, but this time it was softer. Exhaustion was starting to take over. Understanding their situations, and what she must be feeling, he offered a kind smile. With gentle eyes and a soft voice, he simply said, "I'm sorry."

His words didn't solve the problem, but something in his voice eased her frustration. A slight sense of relief and a bit of comfort came with his temperament. She let out a soft, dry laugh.

"How cliché," she murmured, unsure whether to laugh or groan.

They stood outside the room, snow crunching beneath them. The door opened slowly, letting a sliver of outside light spill in to illuminate the first few feet. He held the door open as politely as he could.

She squeezed past him, brushing the snow from her hair. She dropped her bag and searched the wall for a switch. Failing at that, she used the little amount of light from the window to make her way to the bathroom and shut the door.

Their brief conversation in the lobby hadn't erased all the discomfort, but it had offered enough reassurance they would both likely wake up the next morning. Both had valid IDs and credit cards providing some proof of identity. They learned both were divorced professionals traveling for work, each about three hours from home.

She had a preteen daughter, and he had two teenage girls, and it seemed their kids shared more than a few hobbies and traits. Most importantly, each represented themselves as thoughtful and intelligent through their honest, empathetic, and sympathetic conversation.

If they had met under different circumstances, it might have been a pleasant introduction, perhaps one that was even welcomed.

He wedged the door open with his foot, giving his eyes time to adjust before locating the switch. Now being able to look around the room, he realized their situation had not improved.

After several minutes, the bathroom door opened and she stepped out to find him sitting on the bed, his face buried in his hands.

He looked up to see her expression, which fell somewhere between fear and frustration as she also realized there was only one bed.

Despite her expression, he noticed—for the first time—just how attractive she was. The way she carried herself only deepened that impression.

Still, he forced a wry smile in her direction. "Cliché indeed."

Trying to cut the awkward tension before it grew even more, he continued by indicating his plan. "I claim the floor… as long as I can steal a pillow."

She hesitated, then gave a small nod—grateful, though wary of seeming entitled. He had been polite and respectful throughout—both traits she found rare and unexpectedly attractive.

Her frustration faded, replaced by a flicker of unexpected comfort—her first real sense of relaxation. Or maybe it was just exhaustion.

"Are you sure?" she asked, mostly to be polite.

His return smile was enough of a response for her. He stood up and made his way to the bathroom.

As he passed, he gave her a friendly wink, "It's not exactly luxury… but it's softer than asphalt… and warmer than my car. Trust me."

She tilted her head, gave her own gentle smile, and nodded again with appreciation.

Once he disappeared into the bathroom, she let out a giggle. His charm, quick wit, and calm demeanor had managed to take the edge off their uncomfortable situation.

As the bathroom door clicked shut, she pulled out her phone and quietly stepped to the far side of the room. She made a quick call to let her daughter know she was safe, and that she'd ride out the storm. It wasn't a long conversation, but it was an important one. Afterward, she exhaled softly and tucked her phone away.

She kicked off her boots and took her turn sitting on the edge of the bed, taking a moment to slowly rotate her ankles and stretch her legs.

The old radiator finally began to warm the room, its faint hum adding to the hush that settled over everything. For the first time in hours, she felt she didn't have to force the feeling of relaxation.

He emerged from the bathroom freshly washed and barefoot. She was curled up on one side of the bed, fully clothed under the blankets, her body angled away, but not dismissive.

She left a pillow and a folded blanket pulled from the closet at the foot of the bed—his space. It was a quiet offer, signaling she'd let him prepare his place on the floor, but she wasn't forcing him there.

He paused to analyze the situation for a moment before speaking.

"I'm not one to overthink gestures," he said, "but this feels like it could be a trap."

Without moving, she smiled while forcing herself not to laugh. "And yet, you're still thinking about it."

His laugh then allowed her to release hers—soft and genuine. Another layer of tension between them melted away.

"I promise I won't snore," she added.

"I might, but only in self-defense." He took the pillow and blanket and lowered himself onto the floor, away from the bed and closer to the window.

"This is more for me than for you," he shared. "I'm banking on karma to pay me back."

She felt his movement to the floor and turned over to face him, propping her head on her hand. Though his flannel pants and fitted T-shirt covered him, she couldn't help but notice the way he moved. Stronger than most men his age.

"I think the truck driver already gave you an advance on karma," she teased.

"Touché," he grinned as he began to take off his shirt.

Her assumption had been right—he wasn't perfect, but he clearly took care of himself.

"So, I guess this is me paying it…" he trailed off, noticing she was watching him as he removed his shirt.

"Sorry, is this okay?" he asked.

"Mmm," she responded. She meant it as a yes, but the sound came out far more suggestive than she'd intended. Her eyes widened as her cheeks flushed.

Great, she thought. *That's helpful.*

She sat up, quickly grabbed something from her bag, and retreated to the bathroom.

He settled into a comfortable position, popped in his earbuds and hit shuffle.

After skipping a few tracks, he gave in to a familiar keyboard melody and closed his eyes.

As the bathroom door opened, the light lit the room momentarily, indicating her return.

Peeking through one eye, he caught her silhouette against the glow. Now that he was settled on the floor, she had changed into something more comfortable—a fitted sweatshirt that slipped off one shoulder, paired with soft sleep shorts.

Subtle and unintentional, it hugged her body enough while the light caught her legs—nearly impossible to ignore.

The irony of the lyrics in his ears hit him full force.

> *Ooh, and there she stands in a silken gown;*
> *Silver lights shinin' down…*
> *Love comes walkin' in.*

He looked away, telling himself not to be that guy—but it was too late. The image was already etched into his memory.

He closed his eyes and pulled the music from his ears, pretending to be fading off.

She planned the quickest path to the bed, switched off the bathroom light and darted under the covers like a child attempting to outrun the dark.

After a few minutes, he heard her shift in the bed and now felt her presence in a different way.

Curiosity got the better of him.

He looked up just as she opened her eyes and they locked in place.

Not romantically. Not seductively. Just quietly. Present.

A shared pause of mutual understanding—disbelief, gratitude and recognition.

She'd never imagined feeling safe with a stranger, or perhaps that's why she felt comfortable.

They didn't *plan* to be there.

They didn't *want* to be there.

But maybe—just maybe—they were *meant* to be.

PILLOW TALK

The silence pressed in around them. Neither of them could sleep and each of them could sense the other was still awake.

She finally broke the stillness with a soft, "Thank you," just loud enough in case she was wrong about him being awake.

He assumed her thank you was referring to him taking refuge on the floor, but wasn't entirely sure.

Either way, "You're welcome. Thank you, as well," he said.

"For what?"

"For the trust. Your willingness to share your room with a stranger. I don't take that lightly."

She paused for a moment to digest his comment. *Did he just refer to it as her room?*

"Well… I'm not sure I'd call it trust," she continued, "but I appreciate the chivalry."

"I'll take that. I know trust is hard to find these days. And the appreciation is a bonus."

She didn't sense any bad intentions, but something in his tone hinted at something more. Since sleep didn't seem to be coming soon, she gently probed.

"You don't think women appreciate chivalry?"

He paused long enough to make her wonder if he'd fallen asleep or was perhaps triggered into not responding.

Just as she was about to break the silence again, he spoke with careful intent. "In my experience, men face an uphill battle with women… especially with trust and appreciation."

He had her attention now, thoughtful, clearly grounded in something real.

She waited, growing impatient when he didn't elaborate. She bit her lip, stopping herself from pushing further. The silence grew awkward.

Then he chuckled. "Okay… so your silence means you either agree, disagree but don't want to argue, or you're now considering smothering me in my sleep."

"To be honest," she said, "they're better than I expected, but these pillows would suck for that."

Her quick and intelligent comeback made him smile in the dark.

She didn't let her comment slow the discussion and continued.

"I think both men and women struggle, especially the older we get. We know what we want, what we can tolerate, and what we can't.

I was just curious about your story."

"Well said. I agree," he replied.

"But that assumes people have experienced enough, learned enough, and have actually grown because of it.

The older we get, the more we know what works, what doesn't, and the fewer people who fit into that… or understand it for themselves.

And sometimes, if you meet the right one, all those thoughts go out the window anyway. Have you ever met someone who drove you nuts… but then you found those same traits endearing in someone else?

I've been single for a while. I know what I want and what I don't.

But that could all change in a heartbeat with the right person. I'm broken, like most people.

But I *know* I'm broken, and I'll never stop trying. That has to count for something, right?

I'm not perfect. I'm not looking for perfection. But I believe I *might* be perfect… for *someone*."

Her smile froze.

"Wow…" was all she could manage to say. He had just shared more than most men would share in two or three separate conversations. She then regretted how dismissive her response might have sounded. She actually enjoyed hearing him speak, and even more that he shared what he had.

She quickly lightened the moment and covered her reaction with a bit of humor. "You're single?"

"I am," he said, laughing.

"Sorry for the monologue... probably something you should've learned before agreeing to share a room. But yes. The dating pool is either way too shallow or filled with too much chlorine."

"Or not enough," she added. "Would it matter if you weren't single? Sharing a room like this?"

"No, probably not. I didn't see a ring on your finger, but I know that doesn't always mean anything.

If it mattered to you, then it would've mattered to me."

"There's that chivalry again. Thank you.

So what's your take? Why do you feel trust and appreciation are rare?"

"I've probably already shared too much... but take chivalry. So many people feel entitled. They expect it or even demand it.

And honestly, that's fine, I guess. I would be that way regardless. It's just who I am.

But when there's no appreciation, or even acknowledgement, it can wear on you.

It can even get toxic. Many women want to feel like a queen, which is great, because that's exactly how I'd want my partner to feel.

But to keep that going, you've got to make the other person feel like a king... or another queen... at least sometimes.

At the very least, appreciate the efforts that are being made."

"Point taken," she chuckled. "Jesters need not apply.

Have you always felt that way, even when you were younger?"

Silence returned. This time from exhaustion, however, neither of them wanted the conversation to end.

Unsure if she'd pushed too far, she started again.

"I didn't mean to…"

"No, you're fine," he said gently.

"You ask a lot of questions. It's not bad. I actually like it. I'm just not used to answering questions or talking about… me. I'm my least favorite topic of discussion, and usually try to avoid it. You seem to be good at getting me to talk.

Anyway… I was trying to think of a good example. I have a lot of them."

"Would you mind sharing one?"

"Many years ago, I worked part-time at a gym. There was this woman I knew… and really wanted to get to know better, if you know what I mean. Everyone told me to ask her out, but I never did.

We weren't close, but I guess we were friends, and I knew she was going through a rough time.

I felt bad and wanted to be there for her… and I also wanted her to know how I felt.

Her birthday was coming up, and she was turning thirty on the thirtieth."

"Awww… her golden birthday."

"Exactly. When she came in that day, I wished her a happy birthday and asked if I could borrow her car keys.

I had a gift for her but didn't want to draw attention at the gym.

She trusted me enough to hand them over, so I guess she didn't think I was a total creep.

I left two things on her seat.

First… you know those roses preserved and dipped in gold?"

After a pause, she realized he wasn't joking and tried not to giggle.

"Yeah… I remember seeing those," she said, eyes wide.

"One of those. The second gift was a poem I wrote for her.

Long story short… she never acknowledged either of them.

Not even a thank you. Not even as a friend. Nothing.

So, I guess I had the trust… she gave me her car keys, but zero appreciation."

They both went quiet. The silence stretched until she couldn't take it anymore and broke into laughter.

"Oh. My. God. You didn't.

That's either the cheesiest thing I've ever heard or the most romantic.

Maybe both. Did you just make that up?"

She hoped he interpreted her tone correctly and that she hadn't trivialized his story and something he genuinely shared. The darkness of the room provided some safety and privacy but also made it difficult to know for sure.

She turned her head and saw a soft glow from his phone now lighting his face.

"Yeah… I figured you might ask that.

I sometimes don't believe it myself, and I'm the one who did it."

After a few moments, he started again. "Okay, I found it. Brace yourself. Here we go.

> *People seem to travel in and out of our lives,*
> *Much like the ocean and the rise of the tides.*
> *Some never enter, just stand on the beach,*
> *While someone that's special may drift out of reach.*
>
> *Think back to the time you first stood on the shore—*
> *A child with wide eyes, ready to explore.*
> *A beautiful girl, small fingers in tow,*
> *You steadied yourself, unsure where to go.*
>
> *You learned friendships are brief, while some last much longer,*
> *Like waves—some are weak, but the fun ones are stronger.*
> *And time, how it flies—those friendships stood sturdy,*
> *You glance back at the beach and realize you're thirty!"*

She let out a quiet breath.

"Wait… you really wrote this? And then just left it in her car?"

"With the rose," he added, half-embarrassed. "I didn't want to put her on the spot in the gym."

"Or put yourself on the spot, I'm sure! It's kind of beautiful. I mean… bold. But beautiful.

I'm sorry. Keep going."

He cleared his throat before continuing.

"Always remember, you're as young as you feel,
Surrounded by waves, by friendships that heal.
The water stays warm—you don't have to feel older,
Even through sadness, when the water seems colder.

Look back on your past, grains of sand—bad and good,
Notice the flower that bloomed where you stood.
The rose is a symbol of many true things,
But mostly for all the emotions it brings.

As feelings grow cold—the heart starts to freeze,
It's time to create some new memories.
A symbol like this should not make you tired,
It's more like a wave, lifting spirits higher.

So look at this rose and let go of the bad,
Just think of your friends and the good times you've had.
It won't wilt or fade, it has been well-preserved,
Just a small gift, one I thought you deserved.

Nothing too fancy—not a full-blown bouquet—
Just one I picked out for your golden birthday."

By the time he finished, her thoughts scrambled to keep up.

She didn't know what to think first, or which of the dozens of thoughts to say aloud.

She decided to play it safe.

"Are you a poet?"

"I don't think so… unless this counts. Then, maybe, I guess. Writing helps me think, relax, and get my thoughts out, even if no one ever reads it."

He chuckled to himself as a few memories surfaced.

"I forgot about her fear of the water…" he whispered to himself.

"Well, I appreciate you sharing that," she said, "and am sorry it didn't work out.

If you've had a lot of those experiences, I can see why you'd be grateful for at least a little appreciation."

She paused, then gently tested a boundary to see what would happen.

"What was her name?"

"Would you believe me if I said I don't remember?"

"No."

"No?"

"Anyone who would write something like that, feels deeply enough for that person to never forget their name."

She had meant it as a compliment, but perhaps she said too much. She tried to lighten the mood with quick misdirection.

"Do you think you overdid it… maybe just a little?"

She was relieved to hear him laugh.

"Oh, I'm sure I did. One hundred percent.

Hindsight makes it worse.

But I also think if she'd been the right one, she would have eaten that up. Right?"

Her laugh was enough validation for him, intended or not.

"I won't change who I am again… for anyone.

I'm just hoping to find someone who appreciates that kind of effort, even if they don't return it… not in the same way or in the same amount. I'd never expect that.

Just someone who trusts me and allows me to melt their heart, or always try. And wants me to.

Do you think women are still capable of that? What about you?"

She froze. The question landed. It was her turn.

"Me? I don't know," she admitted. "I don't think so. And I'm not sure about other women. I've seen some of the worst in people.

I admit, I have trust issues.

My skepticism is high. I either expect the worst, shut down, look for reasons not to trust, or even sabotage things before feelings ever have a chance to grow.

I don't want a relationship anyway. I have my daughter, my career, a few friends, and my family. That's enough."

She let the silence linger and realized her response might have come off harsh.

Before she could apologize, he spoke up.

"I'm sorry…"

"Oh no…" she began to gently respond, shaking her head in the dark.

"No," he continued. "I'm sorry for whoever treated you *that* badly."

She lay still. Silent. No one had ever apologized to her. Not like that.

It sat quietly in her chest, unexpectedly warm. She decided to share a little more.

"I've met some cruel men. My ex, and his kids from a previous relationship, were abusive… both to me and my daughter.

He was paranoid, jealous, self-centered, and about a hundred other things I didn't realize, see, or admit, until it was too late.

Now I think those are the only traits I see in people, or maybe the only ones I look for."

"Trust is huge," he said. "It can take a lifetime to build, and one misunderstanding can destroy it. Even if no one's at fault.

Communication is critical. Someone once told me, 'Don't bleed on the knife that didn't cut you.'

But it's hard not to punish the next person for what you've experienced with others."

"Self-preservation," she added. "Maybe it will change someday, but I'm not counting on it.

Relationships just aren't worth it."

His heart sank and he wasn't sure why. He had no reason to care.

Perhaps his empathy was doing what it does—acting as a blessing and a curse—depending on the moment. He tried to offer some advice, disguised as support for what she might be feeling.

"I get it. I have similar fears.

We're all damaged to some degree. That's life.

What's sad is if two people meet who are perfect for each other, and they're both too damaged, guarded, or skeptical… to give the other one, or them, a chance."

That hit her in an unexpected way. She turned toward him again and saw his eyes shut.

His voice softened in the dark. "Maybe the right person is out there. Not perfect. Not unscarred.

But willing to make the effort… or at least try… and is trustworthy to overcome our doubts.

And maybe that's enough."

The faintest smile touched her lips.

"Maybe it is."

As her smile faded, a bit of loneliness crept into the bed beside her.

The silence returned, but this time it wasn't empty.

It felt—different. Like something fragile had taken shape between them.

Something neither of them could name.

They had shared more than expected, and while it felt like there was more, it was enough.

Outside, the snow continued to fall as the night deepened.

The world waited, as they both drifted off to sleep.

THE SNOWFLAKE

She woke up alone, momentarily disoriented by the unfamiliar surroundings and the empty floor nearby. A flicker of disappointment stirred before practicality kicked in. She reached for her phone and sighed. Dead battery.

She must have been more distracted last night than she realized. Leaning over the bed, she dug into her bag and pulled out her charger.

The light in the room was faint, barely pressing through the window coverings. It felt later than it looked. She peeled herself off the bed and made her way to the window, hoping for a better sense of what the storm left behind.

But before she reached the window, she heard the key slide into the locked door and click. She darted back into bed, pulled the covers over her head, and pretended to be asleep.

She buried her smile in the pillow. *What exactly was she doing?* But it was too late to back out now. She was committed to the plan. Whatever that meant.

The door slowly creaked open.

"Good morning," she said, without lifting her head.

"Good morning," he replied, his voice warm. "Hope I didn't wake you. I thought I'd check things out and make a call about my car. More importantly, are you a coffee drinker?"

She sat up to see him holding a steaming cup.

"Oh, you're an angel," she said, accepting the cup with both hands.

"Nothing like a hot cup of instant coffee," he said with a deadpan tone.

She paused, taking in the coffee's aroma and giving him a look.

He laughed. "I'm kidding. It's not fancy… but it's the best I could find."

She paused, then started to take a sip with a smile that surprised even her.

"Oh, wait!" he said. He reached into his pocket and unloaded a ridiculous assortment of options, including creamers, raw sugar, Splenda, Sweet'N Low, and Equal. "I wasn't sure what you might like."

She blinked. *Was he serious?* "What, no honey?" she asked in a semi-sarcastic tone.

He grinned, reached into his other pocket and pulled out two packets of honey. "Oh yeah… Ta-da! No steak and eggs, though. Sorry."

"That's okay. You're sweet," she said, stirring in a few packets. "Thank you. Where's yours?"

"Not a coffee drinker."

She paused as her perspective shifted. Her quick reflection surprised her—the quiet tenderness of his act. He'd done this just for her.

Last night they'd barely spoken. Now, he was offering her warmth in more ways than one.

He watched her take a sip, which made him smile.

"Thanks for the trust," he said.

She hadn't even questioned the coffee, and that meant something. As did her appreciation.

"Oh. And it's still snowing," he added. "My car's probably buried until spring. And we're not going anywhere."

They made their way to the lobby, looking for options—and a welcome distraction. An older man stood by the coffee machine, chatting with the clerk at the front desk. When he saw the two, he smiled and wished them a good morning.

It didn't take long for them to realize the storm had shut down nearly everything, likely until the next day.

There was some comfort in knowing they were safe, yet both were wired for productivity. While they enjoyed their downtime, being idle wasn't exactly their thing.

The old man finished pouring his coffee. He admired how the two were handling the situation, and it made him feel good to have people handle the potential negativity so well together. Not like most couples he had seen in his years. It was refreshing.

"You two are so cute together," the old man said.

She laughed, though the words lingered longer than she expected.

"Are you two interested in a change of scenery?" he asked.

She sensed her new roommate standing next to her preparing to correct the old man and grabbed his arm to prevent him.

"What do you mean?" she asked.

The stranger described a nearby resort, about twenty-five minutes away. It was similar to a small ski village, with better amenities and a little more to do versus the motel.

"No offense," he added, nodding to the desk clerk.

She raised an eyebrow. "If I could make it twenty-five minutes, I'd just keep driving."

"Oh, no, young lady," he said. "You're not driving anywhere. Roads won't be open until after the storm. I'm heading back there for work… and I can take you. Just not by road."

He motioned outside.

They both turned to look. She blinked. "In that?"

They both stared. A rugged, tracked snowcat—a sort of oversized snowmobile with a cozy cabin—sat waiting.

"Well, that looks… interesting," her companion said as he turned to gauge her reaction.

She gave him a lingering look in return.

"So, you think I should pack up my things, trust this guy I don't know, ride through the snow to a place I've never been, in *that* thing, with someone I just met last night?"

Fair questions.

Furthermore, he had no real answer to any of them. He simply smiled in return.

"Alright," she said lightly, surprising them both.

She didn't quite trust the stranger with the snowcat—but the 'stranger' at her side? That seemed different.

Was this crazy? Maybe. Probably. But so was everything else that had happened.

It wasn't just the coffee, or the steadiness in his voice. It was something about the way he hadn't tried to impress her. He just made space for her.

She glanced at him again, and he gave her a look. Half surprised, half impressed but said nothing.

There was something about the ease in her voice, the spark in her eyes, that made him trust her decision as much as she seemed to trust him.

She broke her thoughts.

"I just hope I don't hear anything remotely resembling *'Dies Irae'* along the way."

He gave her a confused look.

"*The Shining?*" She laughed. "Never mind. I need to make a call, take care of the room, and then we can go."

"No need, ma'am," the desk clerk added. "The gentleman already took care of the room this morning."

The ride to the resort was unexpectedly beautiful and fun. Snow blanketed the wilderness in impossible stillness. It was full of scenery the highway could have never offered.

Seated between the two men, she couldn't help but notice how she was sitting close, favoring her new travel companion without realizing it.

She wasn't sure when their legs had started touching, or when she'd stopped pulling away. Not just their legs—their feet, hips, arms, even their breath were occasionally in sync.

Uncertain of what was to come, the anticipation seemed to be growing. Whatever it was, they were in it together.

When they arrived, she stood at the edge of the driveway, snowflakes swirling at her boots, the trees rising like cathedral walls. She felt as if she'd stepped into another world. The air was crisp, scented with pine and cold earth.

He joined her, bags in hand, a cautious smile on his face. "Let's get inside before we freeze."

The place was as promised. It was more village than motel, complete with shops, cafés, bars and even a library.

The best features were the secluded cabins which provided just the right amount of peaceful isolation. This time the weather worked in their favor, as the storm resulted in several cancellations.

Their cabin was small but warm. A stone fireplace, an oversized rug, and exposed wooden beams created a hush that softened everything. It was cozy—the kind that invited intimacy.

He paused as he passed a window and glanced out. A pool lay silent, a buried, frozen oasis hidden from view, private and untouched.

She joined him, peering through the frosted glass.

"Did you bring your suit?" she teased as she walked away.

"Don't need one," he replied with a grin. "Looks like it's just ours."

She continued to explore, the question still lingering in her mind: *What exactly was she doing here?*

They took a few minutes to settle in and explore. He stood at the doorway to one of the rooms, eyes shut, shaking his head and chuckling.

"One bed," he said. "Had to expect *that.*"

"At least you've got a fireplace next to *your bed* this time," she offered with a grin.

"Do you *always* look at the bright side?" he asked.

The question caught her off guard. She didn't. But she was. Or maybe she was starting to.

She let the silence answer, perhaps the answer still undetermined.

He ignored the lack of response and crossed the room, drawn by something that seemed out of place on the bookshelf—an angle, maybe, or a faint asymmetry.

As she turned to walk towards the bathroom, she heard the faint sound of his knuckles knocking on wood. *Tap… tap-tap.*

Something caught his eye, and he was now crouched down near the bottom of the built-in bookshelf. He ran his fingers along the bottom shelf until they caught on something. An edge, maybe a seam. A slight indentation that didn't match the rest of the frame.

"What are you doing?" she asked as she walked over and knelt beside him.

"My grandfather was a woodworker. This is hand-crafted. This piece… this corner… doesn't match. It's subtle, different, and I think there's something else here. Maybe not."

"May I?" she asked, gently replacing his hands near the bookshelf.

During the exchange, their fingers brushed slightly against each other for the first time. There was a brief pause as they looked at each other, slightly awkwardly, but smiling.

She let her fingers feel along the edge. After a moment, she felt something. With a careful push, a soft click echoed as a panel slid open.

He looked at her with a grin.

"I grew up with Nancy Drew," she said with a smile.

He responded with a compliment. "I guess you've got the perfect touch."

A flurry of possible flirtatious comments flooded their minds, but the smiles they exchanged said enough.

They peered behind the panel.

Inside the narrow compartment was a small wooden box and a folded piece of parchment. It was dusty and clearly used with purpose at some point.

"Go ahead, Sherlock," she said.

He lifted the contents out. "Well… it's too small for a 'What's in the box?!' reference," he joked.

The parchment crackled as he unfolded it. The ink was slightly faded, but still legible.

> *If you're reading this, you're either lost, curious, or both. Either way, welcome. There's more to this cabin than you may realize. It was built with love, which is the desired wish for anyone that enters. During your stay, stay open for anything.*

"That's kinda cryptic," she whispered, as she lifted the box.

He smiled. "Your turn, Pandora."

She opened the box to reveal three items: an old photograph of the cabin in another season, a flat smooth stone with a strange rune carved into it and another folded piece of parchment.

"Yay! A treasure map!" she joked, eyeing the paper.

She paused to look at him.

"Do you think this is part of the resort's whole… vibe? Like some immersive mystery thing?"

She looked back to the paper as he spoke.

"Maybe," he said, "but that would make us players in a game we didn't sign up for. It doesn't look staged. I think it's real. I mean, it doesn't look like it's been opened in… well… a long time. Maybe it belonged to the original owner."

He watched her hands as she opened the paper.

Outside, the snow continued to blanket the world in a hush of white.

Inside, the fireplace was still unlit, but the air between them felt warmer somehow, charged with something unspoken.

"Oh, you're gonna love this," she said. "I'll let you read it."

She handed him the parchment, and he began to review it.

"Out loud… if you please. My poet," she teased sweetly.

Her comment made his heart skip a beat. He knew how she meant it, but it landed differently and in a spot he hadn't expected, or felt, in a long time. If ever.

As he glanced over it, he quickly realized why she had given it to him to read. It was a love poem, presumably written by the original owner.

"Ah, I see," he responded. "Okay, here we go again.

> *Edlira*
> *My Love, My Snowflake*
>
> *Most view a snowflake as not much at all,*
> *Just something to manage whenever they fall.*
> *They may cause some problems, and yes, can be cold,*
> *But most overlook the wonder they hold.*
>
> *But if you let go, your mind will explore—*
> *You will discover each one is much more.*
> *Take time to think of just one little flake,*
> *The power it holds and the impact it makes.*
>
> *Each one is unique—and for me, it is true,*
> *Because regardless of which, I'm reminded of you.*
> *The beauty of snowflakes adorns any scene,*
> *Like your beauty which stems from beyond what is seen.*
> *Many may see you and stop at your skin,*
> *But your beauty to me is felt deep within.*

You help me feel trust, romantic inside,
And you always amaze me and keep me surprised.
You bring out my laugh and help face my fears,
Take me to ecstasy and help dry my tears.
This type of beauty is a lost form of art,
The kind I can feel from deep in my heart.

A snowflake is relentless, and like them all,
Has no direction but continues to fall.
Each one is strong, enduring weather's demands,
And never gives up, until finally it lands.
You have the strength, the skill and the form,
And have the resolve to weather a storm.

You show no signs of pressure, no apprehension,
And just move along with your desired intention.
No matter your goal, I know where you'll stand,
Successful in all things, wherever you land.

A snowflake is agile, it flies with the breeze,
Just as you adapt to changes with ease.
You sense what surrounds you and shift as you must,
Handling everything with instinct and trust.
You adjust as you go and travel in faith,
Letting destiny guide you, which never runs late."

She exhaled a soft sigh—loud enough to make him pause and smile.

"Uh oh. It's that bad?" he asked.

"Seriously?" she countered. "Beauty. Desire. Strength. Trust. Faith. Destiny. Obviously this guy sees something beyond unique in this woman. It's amazing. Not sure it's real, but hey, a woman can dream."

He laughed at her mild skepticism and smiled.

"Should I keep going?"

"Please do."

"A snowflake is pure, untainted and clean,
Like your beautiful heart, never angry or mean.
Along with your heart, I feel your genuine soul,
Which helps me envision you as a whole.

A snowflake is delicate, fragile to touch,
Like the tenderness in you I cherish so much.
Not one to treat carelessly—honest, direct—
Always deserving a great deal of respect.

A snowflake is sweet like a kiss on your nose,
Or the beautiful scent of a freshly cut rose.
The sound of your voice, the love in your eyes
Only rival your kiss as the ultimate prize.
A snowflake is fun, alone or together,
Like your smile and laugh that bring others pleasure.

With no effort at all, you do what you do,
Spreading joy to those lucky enough to know you.
A snowflake is loved—of course, not by all,
Still a powerful feeling from something so small.
To be loved by the world is too big a demand,
You only need mine, so please, take my hand.

I feel love for you every day that I live,
And cherish the thought of all I can give.
Every snowflake is precious and one of a kind—
A likeness to you, and why you live on my mind.
You are truly unique and special to me,
And likely to anyone who takes time to see.

My time with you cannot be measured,
Instead just appreciated and to always be treasured.
A snowflake now has new meaning, it's true,
Simply because each one reminds me of you.
You're a wonder to value, to love and to hold,
And not just around when the weather gets cold.
It's just how I see you, and how deeply I've felt,
And it's ironic, considering—you make my heart melt."

The room seemed to hold its breath, the silence carrying the words.

When he finished reading, she felt a flicker of disappointment, although she wasn't sure if it was because the poem ended or because his voice stopped.

He had read with a calm, almost reverent cadence, and she found herself captivated by the steady and relaxed tone of his voice.

He hadn't written it, but the words seemed to carry weight between the two of them.

She blinked. Shaking off the spell.

"Okay… a bit less cryptic," she said softly. "That's actually incredibly sweet."

He remained quiet, still staring at the paper. His expression was unreadable.

She leaned closer, gently brushing against him, intentionally, as she reached into the compartment again.

"What are you doing?" he asked.

"It's a great poem," she teased, "but it's not *nearly* as powerful as others I've heard and I was just curious if there was a golden rose, or maybe a golden snowflake stashed in here too."

He gave her a slight, loving push with a hearty, sarcastic laugh that still managed to feel warm.

"Are you hungry?" he asked.

"Starving."

He stood and placed the box and parchment on the desk.

"So much excitement. Want to grab lunch? Maybe do a little more exploring?"

"Absolutely."

He reached down just as she reached up, their hands meeting in perfect sync. He helped her stand.

The contact was unmistakable—warm palms and fingers catching.

The spark sent a shiver through her—a delicious chill, colder than the weather, which no fire could chase away.

Maybe some wine would warm them a bit and allow time to slow a bit more.

BY THE FIRE

After lunch, they spent the day exploring the resort—wandering into quiet shops, laughing at cheesy souvenirs, and sharing stories over steaming mugs of cocoa.

Dinner was at a cozy restaurant set beneath several strands of twinkling lights.

As the wine flowed, their conversation deepened. She found herself revealing things she hadn't spoken aloud in years: her faltering marriage, the fear of being too much or never enough, not being treated properly, and the art of finding the desired balance between independence and true partnership.

He listened without interrupting, his fingers brushing gently against hers, grounding her without words. The fact that this should have been more awkward continued to cross both their minds. But it wasn't.

By the time they returned to the cabin, the snow had slowed to a whisper. Flakes still drifted down beneath a clearing sky, stars just beginning to appear like a silent promise. There was peace in the calm after the storm, with anticipation the only sensation that remained.

They slipped inside, escaping the cold night air.

He was the first to break the silence.

"I can start a fire if you want to get comfortable," he offered in a soft tone, gently gauging her comfort.

"Perfect. It would be a shame not to use it."

She smiled to herself, then pulled out her phone as she stepped into the bedroom. A quick check-in was in order—just to let her daughter know she was safe and settled in for another night.

Now, she could truly begin to relax.

She emptied her bag from the day onto the bed. She eyed one of her spontaneous purchases—a midnight-black nightie and robe. Perhaps she bought it because, for the first time in years, she felt sexy. Desired. Seen. Or maybe it had been wishful thinking.

She tried not to dwell on the thoughts spinning through her mind. As a distraction, she called out with a question she knew could shape the rest of the night.

"Do you want to open one of those bottles of wine?"

Her heart skipped a beat when he answered, "You read my mind. I'm glad you asked."

Maybe they were on the same page, she thought—which made the decision on what to wear a little easier.

She returned from the bedroom wearing her new purchase—and settled onto the thick rug in front of the fireplace. The texture was soft against her skin as she reached for her glass of wine.

"Everything okay?" he asked softly from the other room.

"Yes. My daughter is with her father, but… I like her to know I'm thinking of her. I miss her."

"I bet," he responded as he retreated to change as well. "Mine are with their mom. I texted them earlier… got mostly emojis back. That means they're fine."

"Teenagers," she smiled.

"Indeed. They're funny… when they're not terrifying."

Moments later, he reappeared—flannel boxers, a robe, a slightly nervous smile.

"You look beautiful," he said.

Both understood the respectful yet powerful phrase and how it was delivered.

She felt a warm flutter that had nothing to do with the fire. The mood of the room shifted to one that neither expected nor could remember feeling in a long time.

He paused for a moment then settled in behind her, his legs framing her hips.

"Is this okay?" he asked, sensing his somewhat bold action.

Instead of responding, she leaned back into him gently, until there was no space left between them. Both immediately embraced the comfort they felt, and the shared mindset that allowed the attraction to unfold.

He took her silent yes and wrapped his arms around her. Burying his face in her hair, he held her close until she passed him a glass.

They clinked gently.

"To chance encounters," he toasted, "as cliché as they may be."

They sipped their wine, taking in the warmth, being hypnotized by the dancing flames.

Conversation came in soft bursts, playful reflections on the day, but neither ventured too deep—not wanting to disrupt the quiet magic of the moment.

When her glass was empty, she passed it to him. As he set it aside, she took his hand and whispered just loud enough for him to hear, "I've missed this."

"Me too," he replied, pulling her closer.

The words hung, warm and weightless. It was clear that the conversation might have just ended, while both wondered what might happen next.

His thumb traced slow circles on her hand, letting her know he was thinking about her in the most polite and genuine way possible. His other hand reached up to gently gather her hair, sweeping it behind her ear. She relaxed under his touch and settled her head back against his chest.

Fingers trailed down the back of her neck, adjusting her hair to have a clear view of her shoulder. She sighed and tipped her head, granting silent permission.

His hand brushed the other shoulder, stroking lazy, delicate lines across her skin until she parted her robe slightly, her body warming from more than just the fire.

His palm eased onto her stomach, caressing her through her robe, grounding her. The fingers of his other hand traced slow, reverent lines across her collarbone, her jaw, and the curve of her cheek. They traced her parted lips before drifting down to her neck.

She kept her eyes closed, breathing in the moment, and exhaled with a soft "Mmmm…" giving him permission to continue.

He paused, as if unsure.

She reached up, lacing her fingers with his, and guided him beneath her robe.

His touch was a kind of sweet torment—softly exploring the space between her breasts, over her stomach, back up again—careful, slow, never quite going where she silently wished he would. But she wasn't rushing. Not yet. The warmth of the fire, the hum of the connection, the quiet rise of their breathing… all of it felt like something worth relishing.

She turned her head slightly and pressed a soft kiss on his neck. He turned, brushing his lips against her cheek. When she looked up, their eyes locked—closer than either of them expected. One slight movement and their lips would meet. But neither moved.

They held their gaze, frozen in a delicious tension neither wanted to break. Both realizing that moment, however long it lasted, would be the last moment they shared together having never kissed.

The anticipation was torture—electric and erotic—sensations neither had ever felt this powerful before.

Finally, they gave in.

Their lips met in a kiss that started slow and deepened with each return. The heat between them grew quickly as their lips separated allowing their tongues to taste one another. Her hand slid to his leg, her touch grazing upward, while the other still rested on his arm.

As the kissing intensified, so did their desire to feel more of each other. She turned to face him fully.

They lay side by side, and he wrapped one arm around her, the other settling on her hip. He eased the robe gently from her shoulder, his hand drifting along her skin—down her bare arm, to her fingers, then tracing her thigh, lingering just enough to make her breath catch.

She answered his touch in kind, trailing her nails softly down his back. His fingers brushed over the thin fabric that still separated them. She slid beneath his robe, allowing her fingertips to trace upward from his waist.

He lifted her fingers to his lips, pressed a soft kiss into her skin, then returned to exploring her body.

He reached down to her thigh again, making an extra effort to touch her other leg as well. Moving to her inner thigh, he felt her warmth with another light brush against her panties before returning to her chest.

The teasing built until she could take no more.

She gently guided his hand and placed it on her breast.

His breath hitched at the invitation and with care, he opened her robe.

Their kissing deepened again, as his hands began to caress her with growing confidence. A combination of gentle and firm squeezes and pinching of her nipples paused momentarily for them to pull each other in for a close embrace.

She sat up and helped him remove her robe completely.

As he set it aside, she immediately pulled the back of his head to her, allowing their lips to meet once again.

This slight shift allowed his hand to be close enough to feel the heat of her arousal—wet with desire. The feeling drove him to want more, and he slipped a finger just beneath the fabric to tease her growing heat.

She responded, reaching for him through the fabric of his boxers, seeking the evidence of his desire. As she grasped him in her hand, she could already feel his anticipation seeping through the soft flannel.

He lowered his head to kiss her chest as she arched into him, laying her head back to enjoy the affection. Filled with desire to explore and feel more, he slipped his hand beneath the final barrier, feeling her warmth.

Encouraged, she slid her hand beneath his boxers, taking him skin-to-skin as well. Their first touch of one another brought a pause in their kissing, as they looked into each other's eyes, catching their breath.

His kisses trailed lower—her neck, her breasts, to her stomach—her breathing quickened as she released her grip on him. One of her hands now tangled in his hair, the other traced his back.

Moving slowly, she was seemingly about to burst with anticipation. She nudged him downward, her legs parting in welcome.

He paused to kiss her inner thighs, then hooked his fingers beneath the fabric and slipped it down her legs. His hands returned to her breasts as he kissed his way slowly back up. He let his head rest gently against her thigh, causing her legs to separate even more.

His teasing forced her other hand to join as she gently gripped his hair, urging him on.

She moaned softly as he let his tongue explore her wetness, finally tasting her. His movement was slow and deliberate, letting her body and sounds of approval guide him. He ensured to connect with every motion, focusing on what pleased her.

When her desire grew stronger, she pulled him back up to her. Along the way, he paused to kiss her breasts as she slipped away his boxers and took him in her hand.

Their lips met again, hungry and open. He lay half over her, their bodies pressed together, both aching to be closer. No matter how near they got, it never felt close enough.

She began to stroke him gently, teasing him with her light touch.

Wanting the same, he let his fingers find her again and slipped one inside.

Her breath hitched, and she clenched around him, encouraging him to add another. He moved with perfect pressure, coaxing her to the edge.

She raised a leg, allowing him deeper access.

She wanted more. She wanted *him*.

She guided his erection toward her with aching intention closer to her entrance.

He paused, teasing her, allowing the moment to stretch.

He removed his fingers, allowing her to use his excitement to pleasure herself. Teasing her clit, she nearly let him slide inside as he pulled her closer and released a soft sigh by her ear.

Their kissing resumed with greater intensity, their instincts perfectly attuned.

With him still in hand, she adjusted herself and placed him against her wetness. She reached behind him, gripping the firmness of his ass and pulled him closer.

He felt her warm skin, increasing his arousal and the strength of his hardness.

Knowing they were only a minor shift away from crossing the next threshold, their kissing became even more passionate.

They could taste the excitement—feeling the full power of what they were experiencing. A momentary pause allowed a smile to be shared before their tongues connected once again.

Her hands urged him towards her as he pressed against her wetness. Craving her—he ached for more. They both inhaled the moment of their bodies against each other.

Their eyes met—gazing, asking, answering.

Then, she slowly pulled him inside.

They both stilled for a breath, savoring the sensation. While it had been a long time for both, the feeling was more incredible than either remembered—or maybe this was something entirely different.

He withdrew just enough to return again, deeper, guided by her. Their movements were slow and intentional. She continued to help, feeling him deeper with each return. She urged him on with every touch, every subtle movement against his skin.

The heat between them continued to rise with every glance, every touch.

A smile returned as their eyes connected once again.

He rolled onto his back, keeping her with him, their bodies still joined.

She sat astride him, her hands on his chest and his on her hips.

Their eyes never left each other. Their smiles turned to expressions of pleasure as she began to move—rocking slowly, finding her rhythm, feeling him deeper.

He groaned beneath her as his hands explored her body, gripping her breasts, her waist, her thighs. He couldn't seem to explore or touch her enough.

She leaned back slightly. He was deep, while at the same time rubbing against her clit at the perfect angle under her control.

The pleasure built.

She was close—closer than she'd been in years.

The intensity frightened her, but she held his gaze and let herself go as his hands moved to her hips to help her movements.

She could feel him swelling inside her, heightening her arousal.

Feeling her building, he slowed, urging her to wait with him.

He sat up, kissing her neck, holding her close, breathing her in.

When she began her movements again, they were slightly faster, driven. His hips rose to meet hers.

She clenched around him as he gasped—nearly overwhelmed.

She held him tightly, both of them teetering on the edge.

She leaned back again, placing her hands behind her and resting them on his legs—squeezing them.

The feeling was more than he could handle and he began pushing into her with more force.

Their eyes met again—and that was it.

Their bodies erupted together, cries muffled by each other's embrace of the moment. He felt her muscles convulsing around him as her climax washed through her in waves—toes, legs, hips, chest—everything tingled, alive.

She saw the pleasure rushing across his face. His release came moments later, as she felt him pulsate inside her as he whispered her name.

They clung to each other, their breathing ragged, skin slick and tingling with afterglow.

Not wanting the moment to end, they gradually slowed their motions, allowing them to relax and let their breathing slow.

Breaking eye contact, she gently collapsed onto his chest as he wrapped his arms around her. One hand brushed her hair aside to kiss her temple, the other stroked her neck just beneath her ear.

Their legs tangled together, bare feet touching, hearts slowing in sync.

She picked up her head and their eyes met again. No smile—just an undeniable attraction and connection.

Comfortable. Safe.

The world felt far away as the fire crackled low in the background. Its warmth was no longer needed, yet provided the perfect soundtrack to the picturesque snow-covered landscape outside.

No words were spoken, yet both knew they could easily fall for this person—and how terrifying that was.

Maybe they'd both simply forgotten what it felt like—to be truly seen—and desired.

Either way, for tonight—right now—there was nowhere else either of them wanted to be.

RISING STEAM

She awoke feeling refreshed. She kept her eyes shut, resisting the urge to check the time. As she thought back to the night before, she embraced everything they'd experienced.

Finally opening them, she realized he was gone. They had fallen asleep together, yet now he was no longer next to her. Perhaps he'd been a gentleman, giving her space and had retreated to another room, or even slipped away for a morning shower.

She hadn't heard the water running and the cabin seemed to be filled with a quiet peace.

The thought of joining him gave her a quick thrill, but she flinched at the idea before deciding to stay in bed. How could that thought have crossed her mind so quickly? Then again, she couldn't recall the last time she felt this at ease. Not in a long time—maybe not ever.

The intimacy they had shared on only their second night 'together' sparked a flicker of regret. Then she remembered her younger days.

Hmm. I've made worse decisions with less information, she thought to herself with a small, wry smile.

"Screw it."

The bathroom was empty—but the promise of a hot shower was too good to resist. As steam fogged the mirror, she slipped into the peaceful sounds of cascading water.

She closed the door behind her but left it slightly ajar—just in case. As she stepped into the warmth, she heard movement in the other room. Her lips curved into a faint smile.

He was nearby—maybe he'd join her.

She didn't call out. She didn't need to. If he was coming, he'd come. And if not, this moment was hers to cherish.

The temperature was perfect—hot and steady, calming her body as it massaged her. She lathered her hair, letting the thoughts of the night before and the uncertainty of the day ahead swirl and then drift away with the steam.

She tilted her head back, eyes closed and sank into the moment. The scent of lavender mingled with the steam, wrapping around her like a soft blanket as the water eased every muscle.

The faint creak of the door reached her through the sound of water. She didn't open her eyes—but her body tensed, just for a second.

Then she heard it—his breath, warm and close. A warm hand landed softly on her shoulder. She exhaled, a wave of relief and recognition washing over her.

He was there.

Her thoughts melted into a flush of excitement and arousal. She exhaled, hoping the water masked the sound—at least a little.

His hands worked together to gently turn her to face the stream of water.

As he began to rub her shoulders, he pushed her hair aside to nibble and kiss her hot, damp neck. The sensation of his tongue and lips, warm against her skin, made her shiver.

Moving in conjunction with the water, he made his way around— teasing the lobe of her ear, tracing it with his tongue before moving along the curve of her neck. The heat of the water did little to stop the chills that now stiffened her nipples.

His hands slid down her arms, then back up to her shoulders, fingers slow and deliberate.

As his kissing moved to the other side of her neck, he reached her hands and guided them up around his neck.

Her arms wrapped around him instinctively as she laced her hands together behind his head.

His hands slid slowly down the underside of her arms, settling softly on her breasts. He began to massage them with gentle squeezes and tender pinches.

Even without the physical sensation, she could sense his arousal growing behind her. Ignoring the anticipation, she pressed herself into him and could now feel him.

His hardness against her skin, hot and heavy, sent another wave of chills over her body and she couldn't help the soft gasp that slipped from her lips.

Her hands moved slowly down and around his hips, and she pulled him closer.

The water poured over them both, mingling with the heat rising between their bodies.

He lifted her breasts slightly, and they both sighed together. They shared a quiet laugh, aroused even more by hearing each other's pleasure.

With growing confidence and comfort, she rocked her hips gently, allowing her ass to feel him responding with equal urgency. Her head tilted back onto his shoulder, and as she turned her lips found him eagerly waiting.

The kiss was deep, hungry, yet somehow still tender. Just as passionate as their very first.

His hands moved down, tracing her thighs. She leaned into him, resting part of her weight against his legs, and allowing him to explore.

Even more curious, he moved his hands upward—one settled on her hip while the other slipped between her legs.

He gently pulled her closer, as if the feeling of skin-to-skin wasn't enough. She sensed his eagerness to feel her warmth, and she was slick from both the water and her desire. When his fingers finally touched her, she gasped.

He began to let his fingers massage, driving her anticipation even higher. She reached back. Her hand found him and she wrapped it around his length.

The moan that escaped his lips told her exactly how it felt to him. Encouraged, she stroked him gently as he slipped a finger inside her.

Her breath hitched.

Their lips met again—urgent and open, tasting the passion between them. He gently added another finger, drawing another soft whimper from her.

Hearing the pleasure, he found the spot which triggered the response and began to tease her. She began to tease him as well, feeling him throb in her palm, between her fingers, and against her hot, wet skin.

He brought his other hand back to her breast, kneading her with firmer pressure. Their breathing grew faster, kisses broken by panting—increasing their excitement even more.

With the intensity rising, she guided his free hand between her legs so they could both join in the pleasuring. As his hand got closer, his fingers brushed against his erection as he touched her.

He slipped his fingers out, took himself in hand, and teased her with the tip of his arousal. She released him, only to reach back and pull him against her—wanting him inside her.

Turning her head, she gently bit his neck, coaxing a low growl from his throat. As her hips moved, she felt him at her edge, waiting for her to draw him in, hard and eager.

She arched back and allowed her body to guide him in. A low moan slipped from them both as he slid inside.

He grabbed her hips, holding her steady as she braced herself against the shower wall. The water pounded onto her back, streaming down their joined bodies, rushing over his erection as it slowly continued to move in and out.

Her nipples remained stiff under the heat, brushing against the spray as the water ran off them. His movements were strong and sure, building as he continued to explore and massage her body.

Her knees trembled. His hands steadied her as he pushed deeper, faster. She clenched around him, and he groaned.

The sound of his pleasure pushed her closer to the edge. Nearly losing control, he paused and she took the chance to turn and face him.

The change of position allowed them to kiss again, face-to-face, desperate and open.

He lifted one of her legs, holding it against his side, his hand gripping her thigh. With his other hand, he reached between the two of them and guided his erection towards her once again.

Their eyes connected—intense, burning desire—and she teased herself with the tip of him until neither could wait any longer. He slid inside again, forcing them both to gasp.

Her hands roamed his back, exploring his body before she gripped his ass and urged him deeper.

Their breathing increased, their pace quickened, hips meeting in rhythm. Breathless, gasping, they climbed together.

Her body shook as he pulsed inside her.

The climax crashed over them—seemingly never-ending—until they stilled in an attempt to catch their breath.

She didn't expect it to feel this intense—or this right.

For a moment, time slowed. Any uncertainty or caution had melted away with the water—all feelings replaced by a rare, fragile sense of belonging.

He slipped out as they laughed quietly together, composing themselves. Their foreheads remained touching—their eyes locked together.

Their breath mingled, lips brushing in an echo of everything they felt. He touched her nose with his briefly before moving in. Their lips parted slightly, allowing their tongues to meet for another soft kiss.

She leaned her head back into the water, letting the flow rinse her hair. He seized the opportunity and kissed her chin, her neck, and her shoulder.

When the heat of the water began to fade, he reached down, wrapped his arms around her, and pulled her in as close as he could.

She hoped the feeling would last, but realized it couldn't—or believed it wouldn't. Shaking the thought away, she remained present. The way his eyes looked at her told her everything she needed to know. He was there—fully, completely—with her. She felt… him.

He rested his forehead against hers again, smiled, and whispered, "Good morning. I got breakfast."

She smiled and whispered back.

"And more importantly…?"

"Coffee," they whispered in unison.

WHEN THE SNOW MELTS

The morning passed in a hush, like the breath between verses of a song.

They moved around each other with ease—but carefully, as if rushing might shatter the fragile spell between them. Neither said what they were thinking—that this might be it. Life, already waiting outside, might not be so forgiving of two strangers who'd found each other by chance.

The storm had eased in the night, and outside, the world had already started to thaw. Snow was melting in sheets off the roof as it dripped down the windows in slow tears. The roads had been cleared while the trees continued to bow under the fading weight of white. His car, delivered by a tow truck that morning, now sat outside—waiting.

A quiet signal of what was to come.

It was time.

She stood by the window, arms crossed tightly around her chest, not from the cold, but to hold onto something—or to hold something in. Her bag was packed, sitting by the door like a quiet announcement.

A silence fell—not awkward, just full. Afraid the wrong words might tilt the moment too far one way or the other, she quietly walked with him to the door, hands hidden in her sleeves.

They left to embark on the quiet journey back to the motel to retrieve her car.

Most of the ride was quiet, each lost in thoughts they hadn't spoken—or maybe couldn't put into words. What had started as a chance now felt dangerous—because it mattered. Maybe—because it could hurt, if they let it.

When they reached the motel, he helped her put her bag in her car before they retreated back to his while hers warmed up. The stillness stretched—thick with the words they weren't saying.

She turned at last, eyes scanning his face as if trying to memorize it. Just in case.

At some point the silence had to be filled.

"I don't know what this was," he said, "or what it is."

She smiled—grateful he had broken the silence.

"It doesn't have to be anything right now. We don't have to define it to know it matters."

He laughed quietly at himself. "God. Why does it feel like I'm leaving something I never had?"

"You had it," she said. "We both did. Even if only for a moment. It was real. Something worth remembering."

He reached over and brushed a strand of hair from her cheek. She leaned into his palm, just for a moment.

The sting behind her eyes surprised her.

"I didn't expect anything like this," she said.

"Me neither."

He leaned in, and they shared another kiss. A shiver traced her spine.

Not from the cold, but from the weight of everything they couldn't—or shouldn't—say. Not desperate, just slow and aching, like they were trying to memorize the shape of goodbye.

Less about passion, more about remembering. They weren't chasing the moment—they were trying to cherish it. A memory, unfolding in real time. Not a promise, not a farewell, just the quiet ache of wishing for more.

"I'm not good at this," she whispered.

"Same. And I think I'd be concerned if you *were* good at this."

His gaze held her in a quiet pause, as if he were trying to absorb every ounce of her presence. She felt it as he continued.

"I'm glad it was you."

That undid her a little.

She closed her eyes, and when he pulled her in, she didn't resist. Their hug was long and quiet. The kind of embrace you give someone when you're not sure you'll get the chance again.

When they finally pulled apart, neither opened their eyes.

She eventually reached for the door handle, and hesitated. She pulled a small, folded piece of paper from her coat pocket.

"It's not the whole poem—just the part that mattered most to me."

He unfolded it and saw her handwriting—curling, unhurried:

> *But if you let go, your mind will explore—*
> *You will discover each one is much more.*
> *Take time to think of just one little flake,*
> *The power it holds and the impact it makes.*

His throat tightened.

When he looked up, she was getting ready to step into the cold. She paused and looked into him, eyes bright.

"In case you forget."

This is ridiculous, he thought, confused by the ache forming. It was crazy to think he already missed her.

"I won't," he said, his voice thick. "We'll see what happens. The world isn't that big. We can keep in touch."

She wasn't sure—but didn't want to dampen the moment.

They pulled out their phones and exchanged numbers with quiet, slightly awkward smiles—somewhat shocked they hadn't done this until now.

She finally stepped outside.

Inside, their warmth lingered—in the scent of skin and the soft hum of the heater.

Outside, the world was waking up—brighter, colder, ready to move on without them.

The snow slushed gently beneath her boots. The air was crisp, carrying the faint scent of damp earth and pine. It was as if the forest itself held its breath.

He immediately exited his car to join her as she walked to hers.

He opened her door as they held hands and shared one last embrace.

As she got in, her hand lingered in his perhaps a moment too long. He swallowed hard, resisting the pull to ask for more time. More clarity. Anything.

"Take care of yourself," she said softly.

He smiled in return.

The door shut, and she pulled out of the motel lot.

"You too," he said quietly to himself.

She looked at him in the mirror as he watched her drive away. Her fingers touched her lips, as if some part of him still lingered there.

He stood for a while, listening to the quiet, until her car disappeared from sight.

The road stretched long and gray, but the blue sky had started to peek through.

Inside him, her voice remained.

It wasn't a promise. But it was the start of something.

Or the end of nothing.

SPRING

IN BLOOM AGAIN

❦ ❦ ❦

He couldn't sleep.

Outside, the moon hung low and steady in the cool early spring sky, casting light through the window onto his bed. His mind was restless as ever. Nights like this seemed to be more frequent, and it was even worse when the world outside was quiet, but his thoughts weren't.

He'd stopped counting how many times he looked at the empty bed next to him, forgetting, only to feel the emptiness—more than physically. He hadn't seen her in a few months. Maybe he had never truly seen her at all. But still, something lingered. Something unfinished.

He thought back to the poem they had found together at the cabin and couldn't help but ponder *their* story. Whatever that author had felt—it was powerful stuff. It made him wonder if he was feeling anything similar to that—if he ever could—or if those types of feelings, mutual or not, were simply reminiscent of days long ago.

Realizing neither his mind nor his body would be resting anytime soon, he reached for a pen.

> *It's been keeping me awake, nearly every single night,*
> *Always glaring down at me—it's never shined so bright.*
> *I can't keep from watching this empty pillow next to me,*
> *I miss your soothing face, in that space you ought to be.*
>
> *Since you've gone away—nothing seems quite right.*
> *Now I share my bed with shadows, and a sliver of moonlight.*
> *I want you lying here with me; it can never be too soon.*
> *I thought I felt your touch last night—*
> *But it must have been the moon.*

He paused, pressing the pen against his lip.

It wasn't poetry, not really. But it came out in rhythm anyway—just like his thoughts.

He knew she wouldn't see this. And if she did, it felt like *too much*—especially for someone he didn't really know. But he wanted to.

Still, she had awakened something in him. Something he hadn't realized was there.

He wasn't even sure what he was trying to say.

Only that he missed her.

He continued.

> *Every night I go to sleep, hoping in a dream you're mine.*
> *Then toss and turn and do all I can, to avoid that evening shine.*
> *I thought I felt your brush again—against my face last night.*
> *It won't allow me to sleep, but it always feels so right.*
>
> *Each time my eyes blink open, my heart just wants to scream—*
> *I'm reminded you're not there again, by that mighty midnight gleam.*
>
> *I need you lying here with me; it can never be too soon.*
> *I thought I felt your touch last night—*
> *But it must have been the moon.*

He never sent it. He never planned to.

But maybe it helped him—just a little.

Maybe now he could find a little rest.

He wasn't sure what the morning would bring—only that thoughts of her would be somewhere in it.

She sat at her desk, cradling a mug that had long since gone cold. Sunday morning wrapped around her like cotton sleepwear, soft against her bare legs curled beneath her. Outside, the quiet held steady, like the world agreed she needed space to think. Her apartment hummed with a playlist in the background, matching her mood—wistful and maybe even a little brave.

Spring had arrived quietly—months after their snowy goodbye. Life doing what it does best—shifting priorities, creating distractions, demanding attention elsewhere. She had learned to set aside her quiet yearnings in favor of what her mind convinced her was necessary. Staying busy was her default, and the productivity helped her outrun any other thoughts.

But today, those thoughts were present, and unusually still.

The silence made room for something deeper to surface.

Something more than nostalgia. A subtle, persistent pull at the edges of her heart.

Memories of their time together surfaced now and then, uninvited, but never unwelcome. They kept in touch, but not often and not consistently, which made it easier to pretend nothing lingered.

But it did.

She missed him in the quiet, familiar ache of absence. The kind of feeling that settles in deep before you even notice it.

A folded piece of paper lay on the desk beside her, with several notes scratched on it. The ink was slightly smudged on one corner where her hand had settled too long. Her fingers brushed over it again. She'd folded it and unfolded it at least a dozen times, attempting to gather and capture her thoughts.

She didn't know what she expected, but a part of her wanted to stop expecting anything and just feel. To feel—*that way*—again.

She read the most recent draft.

I've been thinking of you. I don't know what this is, but I feel it. I feel you. It scares me how much I could want something I keep telling myself I don't. Maybe—you. I've spent so long protecting myself that when something real appears, I just want to run. I'm not ready. I don't want a relationship. Regardless, I miss you.

She had been writing down notes as needed, usually when her heart was spinning faster than her thoughts. It wasn't anything meant to be sent. Not really. It was more of an internal confession than a correspondence. Still, the impulse had not gone away or even subsided.

After a long breath, she reached for her phone and sent a simple message instead.

> *How are you? You've been on my mind. Would you want to come for a visit? No pressure. No expectations. Just a chance to catch up.*

She set down her phone, her heart tripping over itself.

His response didn't come right away, and she tried not to read too much into the silence.

When the reply finally buzzed, his words hit low and deep into her chest.

> *Always. And I'm not sure you ever left my mind.*

Her smile was slow, involuntary, as warmth bloomed.

They made plans quietly, unfolding like petals—inevitable, like spring itself. He would drive up the next available weekend.

When the weekend arrived, she ended work early, unable to focus on anything but the hours ahead.

She tried to lose herself in a book but kept rereading the same paragraph—her gaze continued to drift to the window.

Her text to him was simple and playful.

> *Are you here yet?*

A few moments later, he replied with a playful photo showing where he was. He wasn't far. It wouldn't be long now.

Her heart stuttered when she heard the crunch of the tires outside.

She looked up just in time to see him pull in.

The engine's hum began to fade as he stepped out.

Their day was filled with shared experiences—most were new, and yet most felt oddly familiar.

They didn't rush. There was no need. They wandered the streets and parks, slipped in and out of shops, and even ran a few of her forgotten errands. It didn't really matter.

Everything felt enjoyable and easy when they were together. Conversation flowed like it had before, as if no time at all had passed.

The river shimmered with late-afternoon light, reflecting a sky brushed with wispy clouds. Tulips and daffodils nodded in nearby beds, their bright petals catching in the breeze.

She looked at him, surprised by how natural it felt to imagine a future with him in it. Even his voice had become part of her internal rhythm.

"Perfect spot," he said, pulling out his phone.

"For what?"

"We don't have a picture together."

She leaned into him, and for the first time in as long as she could remember, she didn't feel like she had to explain herself.

His arm cradled around her shoulders, and the weight of it settled something inside her. The breeze lifted strands of her hair as she smiled for the camera.

"Got it."

He glanced at the screen, then turned to her and kissed her without even thinking.

It was unplanned but inevitable. Brief. Potent. It left them both breathless and smiling.

She looked out over the water, her pulse still racing.

Don't overthink this. Just feel it.

The city moved around them, but she felt suspended. Wrapped in a pause neither wanted to break.

Any lingering doubts faded, for the moment. Any questions that hadn't been asked no longer needed answering.

He took her hand in his and they continued walking.

From that point on, it felt strange not to be touching. Hands brushing, shoulders bumping, fingers intertwined, regardless of where they were or what they were doing.

As the day slipped into evening, they noticed how hungry they'd become. It was time to eat.

When considering their options, she suddenly realized it wouldn't really matter.

They would be comfortable wherever they went.

"I have a taste for grape leaves," she said.

He blinked at her and let out a slight laugh. "Excuse me?"

"My mom used to make them. Have you ever had them? I don't know. It just hit me. There's a Lebanese place not far. Want to try it?"

"I'm in!"

At the restaurant, their conversation drifted effortlessly between everything and nothing.

The only time their hands parted was when the food arrived.

Even then, they continued to find excuses to reach across the table—a bite offered here, a napkin passed there, or for no reason at all— just to hold hands.

Their eyes locked in silent connection that never wavered.

Eventually, the server returned with the check and a shy smile.

"I hope you don't mind me saying this, but… you two are amazing."

They both looked up at her, surprised and a bit confused.

"I've been a server for a long time," she continued. "I see people. Watch them. And I've never seen a couple like you. You've been in here longer than most, and neither of you checked your phones once. You just talked... and have been looking at each other the whole time.

That kind of connection... you don't see it often. It makes me smile."

She walked away before they could respond.

Still a bit confused, but now flattered and somewhat delighted, they exchanged a brief look, which caused their own smiles to form.

Neither of them could deny anything she said, but it wasn't something they'd expected anyone to notice, including themselves.

"She thinks we're a couple," she said.

He smiled softly, not really sure how to respond, so he chose not to.

Instead, he reached across the table to take her hand once again.

"I'm just happy to be here with you."

Dusk melted into night.

The lamplights in the park glowed softly, catching on new blossoms. The world felt briefly paused, giving them space to just be. Even the air seemed to hold still, as if time itself was making room for them.

They didn't speak. They didn't need to.

Their hands did the talking.

Soaking in the crisp evening air, the city continued to hum around them. Distant laughter, a train clattering in the distance, the whisper of wind through budding trees.

Though they didn't want the evening to end, they both felt the anticipation of what the rest of the night might bring.

As they reached her apartment, she turned and looked at him.

"You really came."

"I did. And you really invited me."

Inside, the stillness between them softened into something safe.

The room felt warmer with him in it.

It was quiet. Enough for them to hear the clock ticking in the background.

"What are you thinking?" he asked.

"I'm trying not to think at all."

"Maybe that's okay." He smiled gently. "I'm just as guilty. I don't mind the silence, but sometimes it doesn't help."

They leaned in, slowly, with intention.

The kiss wasn't urgent or uncertain. It was steady—a promise wrapped in quiet longing.

"What are we doing?" she whispered.

"Trying not to mess this up."

She rested her head on his shoulder.

"Do you really want… whatever *this* is?"

He turned to face her.

"I think I'd like a chance… with you. With us."

She nodded, a wry smile tugging at her lips.

She searched his eyes as if weighing how much to reveal. The words hovered unspoken for a moment—fragile, raw, and real.

"I can feel that," she finally said softly. "I really like you. But…

You should know… I make a terrible girlfriend."

His brow furrowed, believing her comment was subjective, and something maybe she shouldn't assume on her own.

She continued.

"I'm a great friend, a passionate lover… but I'm not built for relationships. They require things I don't know how to give, or maybe I just don't want to. I always end up disappearing or getting swallowed up. I just… don't trust myself with the label."

He smiled faintly.

"Well, two out of three ain't bad."

She laughed, soft and surprised as he continued.

"We've known each other… what, a few days scattered across a few months? I feel like I've learned a lot about you, and I just want to learn more. And I'd like you to know more about me, but I can't force that. You're the first person I've met who doesn't drain me. You energize me. Is that too much?"

She looked at him, wide-eyed.

"No. Not too much. But what does that mean?"

"Meaning… we're able to have conversations, like this, which a lot of people struggle with, and we barely even know each other. I think you're extraordinary and I'm happy to have you in my life. So let's just enjoy our time together… what we have… and see where it goes."

She smiled and kissed him—slow and certain.

"I like that. Okay."

He smiled, relieved a potential landmine had been avoided. They were on the same page, for now.

"Mind if I rinse off?" she asked.

He started to shake his head, then paused with a mischievous grin.

"No," she said, laughing. "You stay here… this time. I actually want to be quick."

"Fine. But I'm next," he said as she walked away.

"Hey," he called to her.

She paused in the doorway of the bathroom, looking back over her shoulder. The bathroom light haloed around her.

"Yes?"

"Are you back yet?"

SPRING REINS

The light of the morning hadn't crept in yet. It was still early. She blinked awake slowly, cocooned in his warm embrace. One arm stretched around her waist, the familiar weight of him behind her. He hadn't stirred yet. His breathing was slow and steady, the kind that came with deep sleep—or quiet contentment.

Their night had been relaxing. No tangled limbs in any rush of passion. Just shared conversation and the comfort of companionable silence. It was the kind of intimacy that required nothing more than their presence together.

They had held each other through the night like something precious, each adjusting occasionally as if relearning how to sleep next to someone.

In the moments before sleep had taken her, she realized how safe she felt in that stillness. Not just in his arms, but with him.

She couldn't remember the last time she'd woken up feeling this steady—not searching, not second-guessing. Just... here. With someone who saw her. Who *wanted* to see her—and know her—with genuine interest.

The quiet in her chest wasn't emptiness, it was peace.

She continued to enjoy the moment.

When the morning light finally began to filter through the windows, she turned slightly and smiled. "Still breathing, I see," she whispered, her voice barely louder than the breeze through the trees.

He stirred, eyes still closed.

"Am I?" he whispered. "Because from what I can tell, it feels like I could be in heaven."

She elevated her voice, amused, and turned fully.

"Okay, that's way too cute and clever for so early in the morning. Even for a poet."

A smile stretched across his face.

"But you make it *so* easy." He kissed her softly. "Good morning."

"Good morning," she replied. "What if we take a day trip? Not too far, just a couple of hours away. I know a great place we would love."

He opened one eye.

"If this 'we' includes me, absolutely. If this 'we' doesn't include me but still has us spending time together, the answer's still 'absolutely.' Sounds amazing."

She nudged his shoulder with a laugh.

"You're ridiculous."

"You love that about me."

"Maybe."

By mid-morning, they were on the road, windows down, spring air pouring in. It was a perfect mix of sun and fresh breeze. The town was quaint and quiet, the kind of place with shaded parks, antique shops, and plenty of fresh air to breathe.

As they wandered past a lagoon, she spotted a series of cornhole boards just beyond a shaded park pavilion.

She pointed with a grin.

"Do you play?" he asked.

"Never have."

He grinned. That was all it took. Game on. They made their way over and he bent down to hand her a few beanbags.

"Ladies first."

It was hard to say what was more fun—teaching her how to play, the friendly competition of the game itself, or the subtle touches they exchanged between turns.

"You're distracting me on purpose," he said, lining up a throw.

She arched her brow. "Me? Never. Is it working?"

"Yes—obviously, unfortunately—but I'm not complaining."

He periodically tried helping her with her form, though the success was debatable.

"Okay, now bend your knees a little…"

"Are you teaching me or flirting with me?" she asked.

"Yes."

She looked closely at the way he smiled—relaxed, unguarded, which made something stir deep inside her. It wasn't just excitement. It was steadier.

Like safety… with a spark.

The laughter and side conversations made keeping score nearly impossible. Neither of them really cared who won. The true winner could be debated later.

Nearby, within the pavilion itself, several chessboards were carved into stone tables. She wandered over and began pulling pieces from a wooden box. He watched her with curiosity.

"How about a different type of game?" she asked.

"Ah, a mental challenge. Should I be worried?"

Her smile turned sly.

"Very."

The game moved slowly, deliberately. A pleasant silence filled the spaces between moves. No rush.

She watched the shadows shift across the board. In another life, this kind of quiet might have made her anxious. But here, now, it felt easy. Even this type of activity alone may have been awkward with other men she'd known. But with him, it just felt right.

"You ever notice," he said, resting his chin on one hand, "how easy it is to be quiet with some people?"

It was as if he was reading her thoughts. She knew what he meant. However, she responded with a desire to hear him expand.

"What do you mean?"

"Like now. Just sitting here. It's quiet and it doesn't feel empty. Just… natural."

She paused her thinking and looked at him, her rook held loosely in one hand, then responded.

"You're one of the only people I've ever met who makes silence feel… comfortable."

"You're one of the only people I feel I can be myself around."

Her heart skipped.

"So. No pressure, no expectations?" she asked softly.

"Just a little honesty," he said, "and maybe a touch of something more."

He met her eyes, and his voice softened.

"I've experienced enough, and have learned enough, to know something rare when I find it."

"Then let's not ruin it with labels or expectations."

She brushed her hand over his. Her gaze shifted with a quiet, thoughtful smile. She made her next move.

As the afternoon sun stretched long shadows across the streets, their pace naturally slowed. They enjoyed a light lunch and came upon a merchant offering carriage rides. The driver was old-school and soft-spoken. This was an opportunity he didn't want to let pass by.

The carriage rolled at a slow, meandering pace—exactly what they needed.

She leaned into his side, not pressed too close, just enough to feel his warmth.

"I'm not used to feeling this… content," she said, breaking the quiet. "Like I don't need to be anywhere else. Or even want to be."

"That's kind of how I've felt since I got here. I like it." He turned his head slightly, eyes searching hers. "You have a way of making things feel… grounded, like I don't have to figure anything out."

She looked at him, her eyes soft.

"You're making it hard to pretend this is casual."

"Maybe it's not," he replied. "Maybe it's just… simple."

The silence that followed was thoughtful and shared. Easy. A quiet understanding. A rare thing for them both.

Their recent exchange had caused him to quietly reflect, and his heart urged him to break the silence, even if just for a moment.

"I like you," he said with a quiet breath.

She turned toward him, startled but not surprised. She knew his comment carried more weight than the words themselves.

"I mean…" He gave a small, sheepish smile. "I like being with you. All of it. I never seem to get tired of being around you. No matter what we're doing… even if it's nothing. That just doesn't happen for me."

"I get it," she said softly. "I think. It's not just the connection, it's the ease."

"And the attraction," he added, grinning. "Let's not pretend last night didn't require a ridiculous amount of self-control."

She laughed, warm and quiet.

"I could tell. Trust me."

He felt himself blush slightly and leaned his head back against the headrest. He wrapped his arms around her a bit tighter, acknowledging her awareness of his desire for her.

"Why didn't you make a move? I mean, it's okay… but I could tell you wanted to," she added with a wink.

"This was my first time in your space. I don't take you hosting me in your world lightly. That matters. I want you to feel totally safe. Completely in control. What we were sharing was good… great, in fact. And anything else… can always come later."

She was quiet for a moment, then nodded slowly, understanding.

"Maybe that's my point. It's not about what we do. It's just… being with you feels good. Never forced."

Her hand found his as he continued.

"I don't believe anyone completes someone… I've never liked that phrase. But you… complement me. Perfectly. I didn't see that coming."

She smiled.

"I like you, too."

Her heart skipped as she realized that perhaps her words may have also carried just as much weight.

Their exchange said more than either of them expected. Maybe spring wasn't just something happening around them. Maybe it was something she was allowing herself to feel again. Steady, gentle, full of possibilities.

She focused on his arms around her and couldn't help but acknowledge how they made her feel. Like she'd finally found where she belonged. It felt like being 'home' regardless of where they were.

As the carriage pulled to a stop she exhaled slowly, her fingers brushing the worn edge of the seat. The simplicity of the day—no tension, no tests—left her comforted and exposed.

Whatever this was, it was growing roots. And for a moment, she wasn't trying to stop it.

She turned to him.

"I think I missed this feeling… even more than I missed you."

He was fairly certain he knew what she meant, but didn't ask. He didn't need to. He felt her intent. He nodded, his hand lightly resting with hers.

On the drive back, the sun began to dip low. The sky was streaked in pink and amber. They were quiet, music played softly, windows cracked to let in the cooling air.

She reached over to take his hand. He would occasionally give it a gentle squeeze, reminding her of his presence.

The memory of the day settled softly across her chest. Not as a burden, but like a promise she hadn't known she wanted.

She looked over to him and smiled.

"Hi," she said, playful and bright.

He chuckled at how adorable she was. His return smile was even bigger.

"Hi," he responded.

And that was enough. No declarations. No explanations. No need.

Their fingers laced.

The silence between them—more honest than any promise.

Sometimes, maybe love sounded exactly like that—quiet, certain, and completely real.

Simple.

Easy.

HELD IN SILENCE

❧ ❧ ❧

She hadn't gone far, yet the soft music made the space between them feel like a world apart. Her shower had been perfect—steamy, calming, and it brought back memories of another one a few months earlier.

Now, dressed in an oversized T-shirt and a black thong, she felt cozy, relaxed, sexy, and ready for the evening.

The day had been unforgettable—the games, the carriage ride, stories and laughter, touching on everything from childhood memories and family quirks to past heartaches and future dreams. All of it, side by side.

Nothing had been planned, yet every spontaneous turn had felt right. The way he looked at her, the warmth in his glances, the casual touches—everything hinted at something deeper quietly blooming.

In the hush of evening—lights dimmed, moonlight spilled across the floor—she settled down with her back against the couch. Stretching out her legs, she exhaled softly, letting herself unwind.

When she heard the shower stop, her heart fluttered. He would be with her soon.

She heard his footsteps before she saw him. When their eyes met, a familiar current passed between them—unspoken but certain.

They smiled, instinctively.

As he joined her, she reached out and rested her hand on his leg, her thumb tracing a slow line along the fabric. Her gaze rose to meet his—those steady, soft eyes that always seemed to hold more than words could say.

She gave a gentle tug at the leg of his linen pants, and he understood. He sank down beside her without hesitation.

She leaned into him, resting her head on his shoulder as the music played quietly around them. The silence between them was full, humming with everything they didn't need to say.

After a while, she lifted her head and exhaled. He turned toward her, searching her face. Their eyes met again. Her smile deepened.

He brushed his thumb across her cheek, tucking a damp strand of hair behind her ear. She closed her eyes briefly under his touch.

His hand found hers, then trailed slowly up her arm, leaving a soft shiver in its wake. Beneath her bent knee, his touch lingered.

He gave her thigh a gentle squeeze, and their foreheads met, their breath mingling in the quiet space between them. Intoxicating.

His fingers traced down her neck, then up again to cradle her jaw. She leaned into his palm, skin warming beneath it.

He brushed the remaining strands of hair away, his gaze steady and full of desire.

His hand slipped to her thigh again. She rested her hand over his. His fingers wandered upward, over her knee and along her shin, pausing at her ankle.

A quiet hum escaped her lips.

He moved closer, touching her face again, coaxing her toward him. She closed her eyes as his lips met hers—firm, gentle, full of quiet intention.

One lingering kiss that held everything. He kissed her forehead next, resting there for a moment, breathing her in.

When he pulled away, their eyes locked, confirming the connection.

She found his hand again, lacing their fingers, grounding herself in him.

As their lips met—slower, deeper, laced with anticipation—he took her bottom lip between his, savoring it.

When she leaned in, he shifted to meet her fully. Passion rose in quiet waves—familiar, yet new. This wasn't a return to a previous experience. It was something steadier. Like trust rediscovered.

They lost themselves in each other's mouths, kissing slowly, deliberately. His hand tilted her chin toward him. She met him without hesitation.

He moved to her waist; she held onto his arm, anchoring herself. Their tongues met again—soft, coaxing, then aligned in rhythm.

His hands framed her face, holding her there—not to control, but to savor.

She pulled him in, closing every space between them. His body grew warmer beneath her touch.

When he leaned back to remove his shirt, her eyes followed. The quiet strength of his frame only stoked the fire inside her.

Then his mouth was on hers again, hungrier now, full of promise.

Her fingers explored his chest as she shifted to straddle his lap.

He bent his knees, adjusting to bring her closer. His hands glided up her back as he pulled her in.

She sat upright, chest brushing close to his face. He kissed the space between her breasts through her shirt.

His breath was hot. She raised her arms, and he lifted her shirt over her head.

Bare now, her breasts met the heat of his mouth. His hands cupped them gently, thumbs circling slowly.

She laced her fingers behind his neck, holding him to her as his lips closed around a nipple—kissing, teasing, drawing it into his mouth.

She gasped softly, arching her body. He moved to her other breast, tongue tracing, teeth grazing just enough to make her breath hitch again.

Her hips rocked gently, seeking more as the rhythm between them grew.

He guided her down to the rug, never breaking contact. She lay back, heat in her eyes as his hands roamed—shoulders, breasts, stomach.

When his fingers found her waistband—silky, black—he paused, stretching the anticipation.

His touch slowly wandered along her hips and thighs. She arched in response, craving more.

The angle made removal tricky, so she sat up, kissed him hard, and tugged him closer.

His lips traveled again—across her chest and collarbone to the softest part of her neck.

Her head tilted, breath catching. "What are you doing to me?" she thought—or whispered aloud. She wasn't even sure.

He paused, eyes meeting hers as she pulled him back to her lips.

The kiss was hungry—tongues meeting, exploring, tasting. Her hips began to move again—slow and deliberate. She could feel how much he wanted her.

His hands slid to her waist, then lower, gripping the curve of her ass.

Again, he found her waistband. This time, she pulled back just enough. Rising, she slipped her hands down his legs. He kept his hands on her hips as the fabric glided down her thighs.

She stepped out, graceful and sure. His gaze followed her every movement.

Before he could rise, she reached for him—then sank to her knees.

Her hands found his waistband. As she loosened it, he let out a low sound—already swelling in her hands.

She brushed her lips across the bulge pressing against his pants, hard and aching. He exhaled sharply, his fingers drifting into her hair.

She smiled, teasing him. Her nails ran lightly up his chest as her tongue traced the outline of his arousal, just beginning to escape the restraints of the fabric.

Slowly, she caught the waistband between her teeth and tugged it down.

Fully exposed now, she leaned in, placing a kiss at the base of his shaft—then another.

When her lips reached the tip, his breath caught audibly.

His knees buckled. She met his lips as he lowered himself toward her.

Sitting back, she welcomed him as he straddled her. Their bodies pressed tightly together. His arms circled her. She placed a hand on his chin, keeping the kiss alive.

Rising to his knees, he guided his erection between her breasts, sliding against her warm skin.

The sensation awakened an even deeper desire in both of them. She reached around to grab his backside and pulled him in, setting the rhythm as his hardness continued to slide between her breasts.

They paused, breathless, caught in a smoldering gaze.

She smiled, winked, and reached down to take him in her hand.

One hand on his chest, the other wrapped around him. Her touch coaxed gentle thrusts from him.

She leaned in, deepening the kiss as she guided him back between her breasts.

Her strokes remained light, coaxing him with both hands against the softness of her body. His face fell into her hair, lost in sensation. He kissed her again, his mouth eager.

His hands returned to her breasts—massaging, pinching. Her strokes slowed as he gasped, hips twitching.

Feeling him throb, she eased her touch, keeping him at the edge. But he was too close.

He took her hands and gently guided them around his neck. He pulled her closer, chest to chest.

She leaned back slightly, grinding against him—wet and wanting.

Her clit caught friction with each sliding pass against the length of him. She felt him swell beneath her.

His hands drifted down from her breasts to her stomach, then between her thighs.

She gave him a little space, allowing his fingers to explore. Her breath hitched. She moaned, shifting her knee up beside his head.

He kissed her inner thigh—then upward.

She ran her fingers through his hair, lifting her leg to his shoulder, opening further. He kissed every inch he could reach.

She looked down, met his eyes, and placed a finger in his mouth.

He sucked gently, gaze never leaving hers. Her moans built, tension coiling between them. She let her legs fall open and pulled him to her for a deep kiss.

Their bodies reconnected—his erection glided between her thighs.

He kissed her breasts again as his hardness massaged her clit, then slipped lower along the curve of her ass. Her breath came hot and shaky.

He leaned back, pulling her with him. She followed, straddling him again.

She began to grind—wet and steady. She reached down to cup his balls, gently keeping him from climaxing too soon. He groaned, tongue trailing between her breasts.

She rocked in rhythm until he lifted her slightly. She pressed forward, rubbing her clit along his stomach.

Then she rose just enough to let him slide between her folds without entering.

The tension grew unbearable.

They froze—eyes locked, breath held. No words. No smiles. Just raw, silent passion.

He loosened his grip but didn't let her go.

Slowly, she lowered herself, letting his tip slip inside.

Their mouths parted in a hush. Her thighs pressed down. He thrust upward.

Chest to chest, eyes locked, they moved together—hips rolling, bodies meeting, each thrust deeper than the last.

He gently lifted her, laid her back onto the floor, never leaving her.

She wrapped her legs around him, holding him close. He kissed her neck, her jaw, her lips. She met him thrust for thrust.

When he shifted, his fingers found her clit again, circling in rhythm with each movement.

Her moans deepened. She gripped his shoulders, her voice urgent.

"Keep going… right there… don't stop."

Her words sent him closer to the edge.

But he held on, locked on her eyes, riding the intensity.

"I'm close," she gasped. "I want you with me…"

That was all it took.

It wasn't just her body—it was her heart. Her gaze. Her certainty. Her whispered need. It was… all of her.

He gave in completely.

They climbed together, eyes locked, pulses racing.

The release was more than physical. It was a trembling wave of passion that moved through them both.

She felt him throbbing inside her. She tightened around him.

Their bodies clenched in sync, still moving, still kissing.

As the storm passed, their pace slowed.

Their breath began to return to normal.

She reached for the blanket on the couch and pulled it over them.

He curled behind her, their bodies still joined, still warm. His arm wrapped around her.

The room was quiet again. Only the sound of their breathing filled the space.

The silence spoke of peace—something deeper than either of them had expected, but something both now felt.

He let the stillness stretch. "It's never been like this. Not just the…"

She met his eyes. "I know. It's not just that. It's… you."

He smiled faintly. "I think it's us. I missed this. Not just touching you. Just… being near you."

She rested her hand on his chest, feeling the rhythm of his heart. "Likewise."

"It feels like we've been circling this for a long time."

Her smile was soft, sleepy. No more words.

He pulled her close. She let herself melt into him—content in the quiet, where everything unspoken felt understood.

As sleep settled over her, her thoughts drifted.

Indeed. She liked him too.

Maybe even more than she realized… or was willing to admit.

TREADING LIGHTLY

❧ ❧ ❧

Sunlight streamed through the sheer curtains, casting soft, shifting patterns across the hardwood floor. She stirred first, blinking against the light, her red Wisconsin T-shirt slipping off one shoulder. For a moment, she didn't move. She listened to the hush of the room, the distant sounds of the city waking up beyond the windows.

He lay beside her, still asleep. One arm was tucked beneath her pillow, drawing her closer. His other hand rested between them, holding onto hers, fingers intertwined. Had they fallen asleep that way? Had their hands found each other in the night—or perhaps in the early morning? She smirked at the thought. It amazed her how powerful such a simple gesture could be.

She turned slightly, studying the curve of his jaw and the familiar creases of his face. It felt strong, yet fragile. Not just him or the morning light—but this borrowed time they had together.

He stirred, sensing her gaze and the shifting of her body.

"Good morning," he whispered, gently squeezing her hand. He opened his eyes to meet hers.

"Good morning," she whispered back.

He leaned in to kiss her, but she hesitated, pulling back.

He laughed. "What?"

She offered a mock-defensive shrug. "Morning breath."

"Should I be offended... or take that as a hint?"

"Oh, no. It's not good for anyone. Except dragons. And to them, I guess it's just... *normal.*"

He grinned. "Well, I've kissed you after coffee. I've even eaten kale. You have great hygiene and perfect teeth. Honestly... your morning breath is probably better than most people's normal breath. Besides, I don't care. Kiss me."

She gave him a look. Skeptical, amused, slightly stubborn.

"Also," he continued, "kissing increases saliva production, which improves your breath. Look it up."

Her expression didn't budge, but she leaned in anyway, kissing him softly. Closed mouth. It still hit him in that place where no one else, or nothing else could.

"I'll take it," he said, stealing a few more kisses. Then he brushed his nose against hers, slowly with affection. "I'll even take Eskimo kisses with you."

She smiled at his semi-cheesy, adorable charm.

The morning stayed light, full of laughter, teasing, and easy conversation. They continued to watch and learn about each other, even through the simplest of actions. They moved around each other like a practiced dance. Maybe it shouldn't have felt so natural. But it did.

In the afternoon they strolled through a local farmer's market, weaving between vendors selling flowers, books, fruits, vegetables, hand-poured candles, and other crafts.

Eventually, they stopped at a cozy pizza café. They leaned on the table as the sun warmed their faces—sharing stories that made each other laugh. They quietly drew glances from nearby tables, soaking in one another.

They walked the long way back, circling the small lake and waterfall in the park.

At a bench, they sat with ice cream, shoes off, brushing their toes in the grass. They pointed out shapes in the clouds, giving them names. Each name suggested seemed to launch a new topic of conversation.

Regardless of what they did, their fingers stayed laced, as if they'd forgotten how not to be.

Everything felt unhurried—even as the hours passed faster than either of them wanted.

Back at her apartment, the breeze drifting through the cracked window carried the faint scent of lilacs and approaching rain.

They sat on the couch in silence for a few minutes, just leaning into each other. The stillness said more than words.

Feeling a shift, they turned to face each other. Something real had begun to take shape. Not just from the night they'd shared, but from the entire time they had spent together.

As they kissed, it felt less like a question and more like an answer.

They remained resting like that for a while. Her head on his shoulder, his hand on her leg, their bodies relaxed as something deeper began to stir. She was still tired from a long week and from everything they had experienced over the past couple of days.

When the stillness shifted, she stood and walked to the window before speaking.

"You're thinking it's time to go… aren't you?"

He didn't answer right away. Just watched her. How she wrapped her arms around herself. How her voice sounded almost too casual, like she was already filing their time away in a sealed box and thinking about what she needed to do after he left.

"Yeah. Probably," he said quietly, stretching but not yet rising. "I guess."

She nodded, eyes still gazing out the window. "Thank you for coming. It was nice."

He tilted his head. "Just… nice?"

She turned and glanced at him with a soft smile. "Okay, very nice. But if there's any poetry about it, that will have to come from you."

He stood and stepped over to her. "Is there anything else?"

"What do you mean?"

"You usually speak whatever's on your mind, but sometimes it feels like you're being more cautious… like you're trying not to leave fingerprints."

She blinked, caught by surprise. Not in a bad way, but more like he'd touched something she hadn't admitted to herself.

He softened. "I'm not asking for anything. I just like knowing what's real."

She exhaled, her gaze dropping to his chest, then slowly rising to meet his eyes.

"It was more than nice… more than very nice," she admitted. "But if I say too much, it might start to feel like something I don't know how to handle. Or maybe something I don't want to handle."

He nodded. "That's fair."

"I like this. You," she added. "No pressure. No expectations. No definitions."

He reached for her hand, brushing his thumb along her knuckles. "I'm sorry if I pressured you."

"Oh no… you haven't," she said softly. "But I can feel it on my own… and maybe it's not fair."

"Maybe you're right, but it's also only 'not fair' unless someone gets upset. And we're not going to define it, right?"

She nodded with a small laugh—part relief, part something softer. "That's the plan?"

"Yep. It's a highly advanced strategy. Stay friends. Laugh often. Embrace the intimacy. Let it unfold. As often as we can."

She looked at him for a long moment. "You're annoyingly good at this."

He smiled, but it didn't quite reach his eyes—the small sting in his heart still too fresh. "I'm patient, and you make waiting feel easy. I know what things are worth waiting for."

She let her gaze speak for the acknowledgment and agreement she felt.

They stood in the fading light, fingers still intertwined. When he kissed her, it was light, easy, asking for nothing more than she could give. But it lingered. Long enough to leave something behind.

"Text me when you get back," she said as she walked him to the door.

He smiled. "Always."

And then he was gone.

She shut the door gently behind him, her back pressed to the wood for a moment longer than necessary. Trying to feel normal and trying not to feel too much of anything else. But the presence he left behind, the memories she now had, made it difficult.

On his drive home, the memories didn't blur in his rearview mirror. He merged onto the highway as the last light of the sun slipped beneath the horizon. His mind drifted, not to the music, not to the road, but to her.

Her hug at the door had been soft, unhurried—but there was a pause in it. It felt as if part of her was struggling to let go, or as if she didn't want to say it out loud.

He smiled to himself. She wouldn't have to. Not right now.

But something had shifted. He'd felt it. Not just in the way she kissed him goodbye, but in how she *looked* at him right after. Still sorting it out, still careful. She navigated her feelings like a minefield she'd tried to memorize. Each step was calculated, but not yet familiar enough to feel safe.

He respected that. But damn, it made him want to stay close, even if he had to tread lightly.

They'd laughed like it wasn't borrowed, like it could be something more, like it could be theirs—and maybe that unsettled him. It hadn't felt like a fling or even just a visit. It felt like... life. Like a possibility.

Or at least like something he wanted more of, which had the potential to add weight.

Timing is everything.

His thoughts drifted to the way she touched him. And of her laugh and the calming nature of her voice. And of the waitress's knowing comments. The way she gently pulled away, not to push him away, but to keep from pulling him too close, too quickly.

She was trying not to feel too much. He knew that. He felt that. He knew he wasn't going anywhere. Or at least, he didn't want to.

Did you make it home?

I just got in.

Thank you again for visiting. It was good.

Only good?

Okay, very good.

FALL

MORNING TIDE

Life continued. Another season passed and it was now early fall. Even amid the noise of routine, it was her silence he noticed most—the echo of her voice lingered in the quiet.

They kept in contact—but only enough not to lose touch completely. Random texts. The occasional call. Even a few brief visits. But it never felt like enough. They each craved more in their own way, both often wondering how much longer things would continue.

As the season turned crisp around him, she was away—on vacation for some much-needed solitude and beach time with her daughter.

The fight between his head and heart continued and was often the biggest challenge.

That night, he settled into bed and thought of her—something that had become almost a nightly ritual. He closed his eyes and began to dream of her and the beach.

The tide crept up the sand—cold yet refreshing—each wave rising a little higher. The water was absorbed into the sand before soaking into the blanket and then trickling onto his feet.

Half-asleep, he curled his toes against the chill as a quiet moan slipped from his lips. The next wave came, and his eyes opened quickly. He shifted slightly to avoid any additional splashes.

It was getting lighter now. The sun was rising above the ocean's horizon but had yet to clear the cliff that towered over the beach. He looked around, taking in the clutter: a lifeless fire pit, empty bottles and cans, and what appeared to be clothing scattered across the sand.

A puzzled look crossed his face as he realized some of that clothing might be his—he wasn't wearing any. The morning air was brisk, but he remained tucked beneath the blanket's inviting warmth. The beach appeared deserted.

He was alone.

And then it struck him—*they* were alone.

As his memory began to sharpen, he lifted the edge of the blanket to reveal a woman sleeping beside him. An angel. Breathtaking—so peaceful, so still.

Memories of the previous night began to flow in—the two of them sharing hopes and dreams before falling asleep in each other's arms.

He'd remembered finding her attractive, but hadn't realized how much the alcohol might have clouded his judgment. She was even more beautiful than he recalled.

He remembered the ease of their conversation, how he'd wanted to kiss her but hadn't wanted to risk the connection they had made.

Maybe now, a kiss would be acceptable—gentle and harmless.

He leaned down and kissed her forehead softly.

She stirred, eyes still closed, as she soaked in the warmth of the blanket with the sound of the waves crashing against distant rocks.

She had been dreaming of the night before as well, fully aware of where she was now—and of the man beside her. Without opening her eyes, she slid her hand onto his thigh and gave it a gentle squeeze, welcoming his soft kiss.

Her touch encouraged him. He leaned down again and kissed her cheek, lingering just a moment longer to take in her scent and the softness of her skin against his lips.

Feeling his warmth and sensing his intention, she quivered with anticipation. Her fingers slowly traced along his leg. She shifted slightly and let out another soft moan, letting him know she approved of the attention she was receiving.

As she moved, her bare foot brushed against his and remained there—enjoying the moment.

Her skin on his, her fingers on his body—he allowed the reality of the moment to wash over him like the nearby waves.

His heart quickened and he felt himself growing erect. He slowly shifted himself away to provide a bit of space to become fully aroused—being careful to avoid suspicion or startle her.

But she noticed. She felt the space he'd created and assumed the reason why.

The chill crept into the void beneath the blanket. Waiting for another kiss, she realized she missed the warmth of his body more than anything.

Her eager hand found his hip, and she pulled herself, sliding closer to him. She felt the evidence of his arousal pressing against her thigh and smiled—just as she suspected. Just as she had hoped.

Her body stirred and she became aware of a slow, growing arousal between her thighs as well. She closed her eyes again and pulled him even closer, her soft hand moving down to gently take hold of his stiffness.

A quiet moan escaped his lips. Her grasp was soft but deliberate, and he leaned in for another kiss.

He moved to her neck, pressing a firm kiss into the crease and drawing a bit of her skin gently between his lips, grazing it with his tongue.

His hand slid to her hip and rested it there as she continued to hold him, her grip slowly tightening and releasing—encouraging yet restrained.

She tilted her head back, prompting him to meet her gaze. When their eyes met, neither wanted to look away.

A smile formed on his face, answered by hers.

With that silent understanding, she pulled him close, and their lips met—deep and urgent. She separated her lips, feeling his eager tongue wanting to taste her.

Her grasp became a bit more playful as she gently guided his erection toward her.

His hands moved down her backside, and with his touch, she arched toward him, pressing her breasts against his chest.

Overwhelmed by the building desire, she rolled onto her back. She released her grip and reached around to pull him completely on top of her.

Her hair was displayed across the blanket like a fan of silk. Everything about her in that moment felt effortless—undeniably perfect.

He could feel the warmth and softness of her body everywhere. His hands explored her curves as her legs wrapped around him.

Squeezing and tugging, she wanted him closer. She felt the firmness of his desire pressing into her thigh and it took all his strength not to slip inside her.

She wanted him—badly.

Her fingers dug into his back and threaded through his hair as she licked his lips and looked into his eyes.

Her legs pulled him closer until she felt the tip of him press against her entrance—wet with desire.

He kissed her again, harder this time. Their tongues met and he slowly pressed his hips forward and slid inside her.

They both released a breathless moan of ecstasy.

The feeling of him inside her only made her want more. Her body tensed and pulsed, already dancing on the edge of climax with a growing desire for him to release as well.

She met his eyes again and held his gaze, savoring the passion rising between them.

He moved deeper and faster, as she wrapped her arms around him, her legs still holding him close.

He could feel her begin to contract around him, and the sensation pushed him closer to the edge.

Intensity built. Her breath quickened. Moans escaped his lips in rhythm with hers.

As their eyes met again, smiles spread across their faces just before they tipped into their release.

His body tensed and she felt him pulse. The wave started in her toes and rippled upward as they surrendered together.

Breathless, tangled, and overwhelmed, they embraced tightly with another gasp of pleasure.

The passion softened, slowly.

They lay side by side, gazing at each other before turning their attention to the sea.

In that quiet, where breath meets waves and warmth meets skin, something lingered—beyond touch.

Their breathing steadied as they continued their embrace. A few soft kisses followed, only interrupted as their growing smiles met.

The sun had risen over the cliff, casting new warmth onto the blanket draped over them.

They pulled each other closer and tucked themselves deeper underneath as the soft hush of waves filled the morning air.

They were alone on the beach—together.

He slowly opened his eyes.

He'd never been so grateful that he hadn't woken during a dream and that he could still remember every detail.

Lying still and reluctant to move, he felt his heart still pounding with the memory of her touch.

The room was dim, and far from the warmth of the sand and the sun—but her presence remained.

Not in his chest. Not in his bones.

But in his heart.
He reached for his phone out of habit.
Nothing new. No messages.
Just the memory of a dream that felt dangerously real.
He closed his eyes again to savor the moment, as long as he could.

DISTANT SHORE

He began to stir beneath his sheets, the distant echoes of crashing waves still vivid in his mind. Sunlight streamed through the curtains—warm and insistent.

He continued to keep his eyes closed, holding onto the fragments of his dream before they faded: the softness of her skin, the way the salt air mingled with her scent, the effortless way their bodies fit together.

It had only been a dream, but the longing it stirred was unmistakably real. Too real.

His fingers grazed the empty space beside him as if tracing the memory of her warmth. Once again, the ache of absence settled deep in his chest. He took a deep breath and exhaled as much as his body allowed.

He sat up slowly, pushing away the covers. He ran his fingers through his hair as a quiet, half-laugh escaped him—part disbelief, part bittersweet yearning.

Was it foolish to hold on to something born in sleep—or simply the truest of feelings he was being forced to face?

Still caught in the warmth of that imagined morning, he unlocked his phone with the intention, once again, to capture his feelings before they faded.

He hesitated. What if it was too much or too soon? Then again, when had silence ever said what the heart meant—or failed—to say?

His thoughts blurred into verse, part wish, part memory, as his thumb hovered over the blinking cursor, waiting.

Words spilled out—raw, unpolished, yet undeniably meant for her.

You've never been close and now seem out of reach,
As I picture you smiling somewhere at the beach.
Maybe a snack or a drink in your hand—
I sit here and smile and think of you on the sand.

He paused, fingers hovering over the screen, questioning whether or not to keep going.

Vulnerability was a strange beast—equal parts terrifying, brave, and necessary.

But the truth was clear in his heart, and it poured out with steady rhythm.

I'd love to be with you, to escape for a while,
Instead, I open your photo to get a glimpse of your smile.
In awe of your beauty—no one else can compare—
I pause for a moment and imagine I'm there.

Touching the sand—it feels soft like your skin,
I picture you dancing like palms in the wind.
I imagine your scent in the fresh ocean air,
And the water that flows like the waves in your hair.

The words came easily—again, too easily.

It reminded him, unfortunately, of another poem. A different beach. One with a golden rose. That poem hadn't ended in connection, just more distance.

And yet, here he was again. Writing. Reaching.

His eyes drifted to the window, where sunlight spilled across the floor in golden pools.

He could almost feel the warmth of the light, the gentle breeze, the calmness she carried with her.

He took a deep breath, refocused his eyes, and continued.

Reflecting the sun and the clearest blue skies,
No light can compare to the spark in your eyes.
The sun and its brightness, like your radiant face—
With its warmth, I can almost feel your embrace.

The poem and his mission had become more than just words—it was a quiet confession. A hope stitched between stanzas.

The ache of memories and distance softened at the thought of their connection. Was it real?

These thoughts and emotions—all of them real—
And how much I miss you is painful to feel.
Yet with thoughts such as these, I could stay 'here' forever,
Though I'd never think twice unless we were together.

I trust in myself, for my feelings are true,
My mind wanders again, always returning to you.
I focus on us and how you've captured my heart,
And rejoice that no distance will ever keep us apart.

He read over the poem again, feeling the weight of each line—the honesty behind his words.

Again, was it too much? Probably.

He'd felt this before, yet not ever this strong. He'd also taken similar leaps—and they rarely ended well.

Then, almost without thinking, he lay back on the bed and took a selfie—making sure it felt, and looked effortless, natural.

Sunlight cast soft shadows across his face.

A quiet smile lingered on his lips, the vulnerability in his eyes lay bare.

He attached the photo.

Pasted the poem and hesitated.

No caption. No explanation.

He hit send.

And waited.

QUIET REFLECTIONS

She couldn't get his message out of her mind. If she was honest with herself, she wasn't sure she wanted to—or even whether she should.

The time away with her daughter had been wonderful, as always—full of sun, laughter, and much-needed relaxation. But something felt different—a faint tug in her chest, a quiet ache she couldn't explain.

She told herself it wasn't him she was missing, but part of her wasn't so sure.

Especially now.

Her daughter had fallen asleep hours ago, curled beneath an oversized blanket. The quiet rhythm of her breath still lingered in the room.

Now, with the lights low and the rental unit finally quiet, the night offered her something rare: a moment entirely her own.

She reached for her phone, almost without thinking. His message—his poem, his picture—not forgotten. Her eyes scanned the lines once more, this time slower, letting the rhythm of his words settle into her skin. Longing, tenderness, restraint.

It felt like he'd written it with one person in mind.

Her.

She exhaled. This was *not* part of the plan.

She had built her life carefully, deliberately—around her daughter, her career, the quiet discipline of forward motion. She didn't need complications. She certainly didn't need someone slipping under her skin in a way she hadn't expected, hadn't been looking for and hadn't asked for.

She had her career, her goals, her daughter's well-being. Everything else was supposed to come second—if it came at all. She knew relationships could derail everything. And she'd worked too hard to build something stable. Something hers.

But he was there, anyway. In the quiet. In the spaces she tried to fill with other things. And she was letting him in—just a little. In texts, in late-night memories, in the place between resistance and surrender.

She set her phone down and rubbed her bare arms, suddenly aware of the cool night air against her sun-warmed skin. She was still in her T-shirt and underwear from her post-beach shower.

It made her think. She'd been *burned* before, more than once. Lied to. Left behind. Betrayed. Each scar tucked quietly beneath the surface of her carefully composed and protected life.

At one point, she had promised herself she wouldn't let anyone close to her daughter again—she might have even said as much to him. That part of her world was sacred. Off-limits.

But now…

Now there was this man. The risk of letting him in, even if only in glimpses.

She hadn't planned on feeling this way, or maybe she didn't even know how. But the connection they shared was unlike anything she'd known before—unexpected and stirring something she'd long tried to suppress.

Quiet, patient, persistent, fragile—but real.

Despite everything, there was a whisper inside her—a tentative voice urging her to lean in, to risk the unknown.

Maybe she didn't need to have it all figured out.

Maybe wanting something didn't have to mean giving up everything.

Maybe this time—it could be different.

Her eyes drifted back to the phone. She picked it up again to find his photo.

She was drawn to his smile, the glimpse of his chest, the subtle confidence in his gaze. She bit her lip, imagining him there, just beyond the glass—nearly a touch away.

She smiled softly, caught between amusement and curiosity.

How many photos had he taken before sending *this* one?

She could tell he'd taken the time to get it just right—his pose, the angles, the unseen details hidden in the shadows—and under the covers. He'd left just enough for her imagination.

Had he taken the picture with her in mind? Her breath hitched.

Had he been caught up in the moment just as she was now?

The thought warmed her, sparking something low and steady inside.

She stood up.

Her legs moved before her mind caught up, carrying her down the hall. The floor creaked beneath her feet as she reached the bathroom. The gentle click of the lock was like closing out the world behind her.

She glanced at the mirror.

The woman staring back looked like someone she hadn't really seen in a while.

Bare. Honest.

Her sun-kissed skin glowed faintly under the low light. Her eyes, though tired, held something else. Something open. Something quietly hopeful.

She gazed at her reflection, searching for clarity in who she saw, the soft light revealing the layers beneath her calm exterior. A woman both strong and guarded. Shaped by years of lessons, some of them very painful.

Her fingers brushed the cool glass of the mirror, grounding herself in the moment. For now, she would let the hope grow—quietly, cautiously—as she stepped closer to whatever this could become.

She touched her collarbone lightly, as if reaching for the parts of herself she feared might have been missing—the parts she hoped were still there.

Her hand fell to the counter as her fingers gently grazed the smooth surface of her phone.

She wanted to reply to his message, but what could she say? What *should* she say?

A simple "thank you" felt too small.

Something honest? Something playful?

An idea began to form—quiet, but steady. Not reckless—but a subtle invitation. Something to keep his imagination wandering.

She thought about sending a photo of her own—subtle, suggestive enough to stir his thoughts.

To maybe encourage and inspire.

The idea of him finding his own pleasure, holding her image in his thoughts, and feeling the weight of her presence even from afar, stirred something deeper inside.

She lifted her phone and framed a shot in the mirror—subtle and tasteful.

Soft lighting caught the fabric as it hugged her curves in all the right places.

She felt the smoothness of the fabric against her skin, moving with her every motion. Even the thought of him looking at her the way he does brought more confidence than she normally allowed herself.

She snapped the picture.

She didn't send it—not yet. But the thought of his reaction—him seeing her this way—made her heart race. It felt as if it would arouse them both.

She let her hands wander lightly, imagining his touch, the quiet intimacy of a moment shared between two people separated by distance but connected by longing. She let her imagination continue, tasting the warm anticipation like a slow, sweet breath against her skin.

His hands traced gentle paths down her body.

The sound of his voice. His eyes holding hers, focused and attentive.

The way they linger when he looks at her, like she is the only person in the room—or in the world.

As she slid a finger beneath her panties, she turned to take another photo.

She closed her eyes to imagine it was his finger.

Even more—what if he was behind her, gazing at them both in the mirror?

Despite the warmth of the room, his hands sent shivers down her spine, penetrating deep into the cool ceramic floor. Behind her, a few more of his fingers slid deeper, pulling her closer, his growing need pressing against her backside.

His desire became more obvious, as did the hesitation to satisfy the urge. He began to sway gently, caressing himself against her, through the thin layer of fabric.

Leaning forward against the sink, she let herself feel the memory—the possibility—the rare, delicate trust that comes with opening up to someone. She let go without hesitation, fully present to enjoy the moment and embrace the vulnerability.

The teasing warmth, the quiet tension winding through her muscles, the ache of wanting—familiar yet still feeling new.

She imagined what might come next—soft touches, gentle caresses, whispered words—and how he might respond.

The growing anticipation allowed her to continue drifting in the moment.

His hands slid down her front, fingers exploring, teasing—drawing out the moisture already beginning to form. The intensity increased as he pushed a little harder from behind.

As he continued to explore, his hands retreated behind her, allowing her to feel the heat of his palms against her backside. Tugging the fabric down, she could anticipate feeling his firmness against her bare skin.

Knowing him as she did, or maybe as she hoped, he would coax her panties down—trailing them as they reached the floor together. From his knees, he would look up at her while sliding her feet free. After that, the possibilities seemed endless.

The thought of his hands sliding back up her body, slipping under her shirt to cup her breasts, opened even more possibilities. She could feel him growing hard against her leg, craving her.

She imagined the tip of him—glistening, aching, and seeking attention from her, which sent another chill through her. She decided to provide herself with a bit of the pleasure she had been craving.

And then—

A soft knock interrupted the stillness, followed by a drowsy voice just outside the door.

"Mom… are you in there?"

Her eyes opened.

The spell unraveled, not abruptly—but gently, like waking from a dream.

"I'll be right out, babe," she called back softly, adjusting her shirt and smoothing her breath.

She glanced once more at the mirror, not in shame, but with a quiet smile.

What she'd felt didn't disappear—it simply waited.

They would return home tomorrow.

But tonight, she was still there—both mother and woman.

Along with a whisper of what was, what is, and what could be.

SAVING SPACE

Her trip had been wonderful, but it was good to be home.
She sat quietly in the dim glow of her laptop, the soft vibration of the ceiling fan the only sound breaking the stillness. Her daughter lay curled up in bed, deep in the type of sleep that only childhood can summon. It should've been a peaceful moment—a brief opportunity to catch up on work. And it was, on the surface, but inside, something continued to stir.

His message. That poem. It had lodged itself in her mind—like a song she couldn't stop humming, or a feeling she couldn't shake. Should she? Did she want to? Why was she even trying? She hadn't responded yet. Not because she didn't want to, but because she wasn't sure how.

From the start, she'd known the physical attraction had always been there. It had pulsed beneath the surface of every glance. Every look. Every touch—intentional or accidental—every late-night word spoken and each message sent just a little too softly. That part didn't surprise her.

What surprised her was the friendship that followed. The way he listened, the way he understood her words as well as her silence. The way he embraced and adored her quirks, and his never-ending eager and chivalrous behavior. How he was always filled with interest—in her, and every part of her life—along with the care and respect they shared for each other. All of it—unexpected, true and genuine.

And now, something even deeper had started to take shape—an undeniable chemistry. Emotional. Intimate. Undeterred by distance or time. Neither seemed to affect what she felt.

Perhaps that's what scared her.

That kind of chemistry had the power to pull her into something she didn't want—something real. And anything *real* was always risky, because it would likely need to be defined.

She had built a life with careful control. After what she'd been through, trust was something she rationed carefully, never given freely. If ever. She trusted herself, her instincts, and her ability to build and protect the life she and her daughter wanted—and thought they needed.

Everything else—especially relationships, let alone love—felt too dangerous. Too many complications—real, perceived, or imagined.

But with him, the lines were starting to blur. No one else had ever made her feel this seen, this desired. No one else had made her want to stay connected, regardless of whether the connection even existed.

She'd met plenty of men who were interested. Plenty who pursued. Yet none who stayed in her mind like he had. Quietly. Patiently. Without pressure. And seemingly for all the right reasons.

She reached for her phone and stared at his last message. The words weren't just sweet. They were considered, honest and totally him. Her poet. They had stirred something deep inside, something that wanted to be acknowledged or even appreciated.

Her fingers stroked the glass, and the words came faster than expected. It wasn't perfect, but hopefully soft enough to convey how his message made her feel.

> *That's beautiful. Thank you. Thinking of you.*

Sent.

She paused, bit her lip. It wasn't enough. A soft exhale followed as she continued.

> *I'm still not sure how to feel about things, but I really enjoy our time together. I miss it. How are you?*

She hesitated, her thumb hovering over the screen.
Sent.

She closed her eyes the moment the message left her phone. Not in regret—in release.

A few minutes later, his reply arrived.

> *Thinking of you, too. I don't want to change your life, just enhance it if I can, and if you want.*
> *Overall, I'm fine. You? How was your trip?*

She smiled softly, setting the phone aside. The night around her deepened, quiet and full of unspoken promises. She didn't know where this was going. But for the first time in a while, she wasn't running from the feeling. She was cautious but curious.

She grabbed her phone again, *loving* his message, and responded.

> *It was great, thank you for asking. I'm good as well. Just tired. Let's connect later. Good night, handsome.*

He leaned back against the headboard and exhaled, his phone still in hand, eyes locked on their messages. He'd half expected silence, or maybe just a polite *thank you*. Full stop.

Instead, her words lingered. Soft. Careful. Honest. Cautious, but open. It wasn't a confession or a green light, but to him, it meant something. Her efforts always did.

He ran a hand through his hair, a slow smile tugging at his lips. She had always intrigued him with a complicated blend of fierce independence along with a quiet ache for companionship beneath the surface.

But how long would that feeling remain one of intrigue? Even now, he couldn't help but wonder—was he the only one feeling this? Was there something she wasn't saying? Was there someone else, or even more than one? There had always been parts of her world he was never invited into, and he wasn't sure that would ever change. Her guardedness had always made sense to him… but it didn't mean questions didn't arise or continue to linger.

He knew where she stood: skeptical, focused on her priorities, and not looking for complications. He understood and respected all of that—deeply.

From the moment they met, he'd felt a pull. Sure, the physical attraction had been instant. Undeniable. But that attraction became stronger with what came after: the effortless laughter, the shared comfortable silences, the honesty that surfaced when neither of them expected it. Their friendship.

The vulnerability he felt—and wanted to explore—had surprised him and stayed with him.

And now, he couldn't imagine being without it—without her. He refused to feel guilty about wanting more—in volume or frequency. Even if only to see what might develop—or dissolve. Either way—they would at least know.

Still, on nights like this, uncertainty would often creep in.

Was he enough? Was he just a placeholder—or someone to fill a gap, not even a thought in her potential future? Was he just a comfort or convenience? That thought unsettled him, not because it shook his desire, but because it reminded him how much he truly wanted her to share the desire to explore the potential—regardless of the outcome.

She hadn't pulled away. Not completely. And that meant something.

He knew she didn't trust easily. Her past clung to her like armor. Always present, always between her and the rest of the world. Still, she'd let him close enough to feel something real.

Since his divorce, he'd met plenty of women. Each one was different, each with her own unique qualities. Yet none of them made him feel *this* way. Like she carried a piece of him around with her, without realizing it.

His heart, his story, some piece of his future he hadn't dared think about until now. And that scared him more than he wanted to admit.

Not only because he didn't accept it… but because he wanted it. And part of him wished she could embrace that feeling, that fear, as well.

However, that wasn't his choice, and he knew that all too well—a common theme from his past.

He could find someone if he didn't want to be alone—he'd had the chance to court other women more than once. But that wasn't the point. He wasn't searching for someone. He was drawn to her. Not because it was easy, but because it was rare. Worthwhile. Real. *Or so he thought—or felt.* How could it be truly special, if it felt to be one-sided?

Still, he smiled. That uncommon, unguarded smile—starting somewhere deep and rising without permission. Her messages were simple, but from her—to him—they meant more than just the words.

Chemistry like this was rare indeed—if it ever came at all. Never something to take for granted.

She wasn't ready for more, and perhaps she never would be. But for now, she was still showing up in the quiet ways she knew how.

Maybe someday her *life* would shift—allowing space for someone special to be let in.

Maybe someday her *heart* would soften—enough for her to truly *want* someone by her side.

Maybe someday someone would earn her trust, help her shed that armor, and join her in whatever might be possible.

Regardless of what the future held, he wanted to be there—if any of those things ever happened, or to be the one to help *make* them happen.

Then again, maybe things would simply stay the same as they had been since the day they met.

He knew his heart too well, and while he wouldn't want to change it, it came with challenges.

These feelings were becoming familiar, and a few thoughts entered his mind.

Was he chasing someone who wanted to be pursued, but never caught?

Was he falling in love with someone who didn't want to be loved?

Or even worse—

Had he already fallen in love—with the potential—but not the reality?

She clearly had feelings for him—their bond was undeniable—but her desire for a future remained uncertain.

There's nothing more painful than being with someone who doesn't want to lose you—but doesn't want to love you.

He buried his thoughts, knowing there was nothing he could do.

The outcome would reveal itself—over time, one way or another.

He would hold to his desire, and his strength, to be patient—knowing even patience has its limits.

Still, his feelings for her weren't likely to fade. Not unless she forced them to.

Until then, he would remain grateful she was in his life. And for now, that was enough.

Good night, beautiful.

Sent.

He set the phone on the nightstand and let his eyes drift shut.

Her words still hummed in his chest—like something unfinished.

Not broken.

Not lost.

Just waiting.

FALLING SLOWLY

Late fall had arrived, and the chill in the air deepened. Most of the leaves had surrendered to the season's quiet insistence, drifting down to carpet the ground.

Their desire to spend time together never faded, but life kept filling the spaces with other priorities. Like the falling leaves, they often wondered if it might be best to simply let go—and cherish their memories. It was an ongoing battle—whether to hold on and wait for something to change, or to accept that their 'something' had yet to be clearly defined and might never be.

Since her vacation, the pull between them had resurfaced with a familiar force. Perhaps with time, the ache would dull if the pull was left unmet. Until then, hope lingered—vague, fragile, but real.

Work was going to bring him closer to her city for a few days, and the possibility of connecting felt like both a gift and a potential complication. Getting together strictly out of convenience felt at odds with the depth of their bond. He believed even minimal effort could allow their connection to grow into something stronger. It was at least something worth exploring to see if they would continue to develop or not.

He debated reaching out, torn by the cliché: *right person, wrong time.* After all, for the right person, you make time—and want to. But if the timing isn't right, it can't be forced. And if someone won't—or simply doesn't want to make the time, maybe they're not the right person after all. It was one of the reasons defining their relationship felt so difficult—maybe even impossible—and another reason it felt safer not to try.

For now, the only thing that mattered was how he felt.

Selfish, perhaps—but he had paid his dues. The lessons he'd learned had left him with both the desire and the strength to never give up. Like his empathy, that was a trait which could often be both a blessing and a curse.

Besides, the heart wants what the heart wants.

Which may not always be a good thing.

She had always been honest about her view on relationships, yet he remained uncertain about how she truly felt—specifically about the potential they may or may not have.

His feelings began to shift—from the anxiety of not knowing where he stood, to the frustration of not understanding why.

Despite everything, there was no denying the physical attraction, the friendship they'd built, and intimate chemistry they shared.

He made the decision to reach out.

It didn't take long. They would get together, again, during his upcoming visit.

The air now carried a crispness that crept through his sleeves as he waited beneath the golden trees outside the café. Leaves swirled in lazy spirals on the sidewalk, collecting in corners like quiet reminders of the year slipping past.

He glanced at his phone. Not out of impatience, but habit. She had said ten minutes. It had been twelve. Then twenty. Then thirty. He wasn't nervous, but something fluttered in his chest—like the leaves around him. Unsettled but not unpleasant. A kind of quiet anticipation he hadn't felt in a long time.

Then he saw her.

"You waited," she said, a touch out of breath.

"Always," he said, trying to sound casual, but his voice gave him away. "I also didn't have anywhere else to be right now."

She reached him, giving a quick kiss and embrace. Her eyes softened. "I'm glad. I'm sorry I'm late. You look great."

"So do you. Beautiful, actually. It's good to see you."

"Likewise."

They walked without a plan, the activity in the streets passing time around them. Conversation still came easily, yet there seemed to be a bit of coolness this time, much like the weather around them.

Yet, they still moved together like two people who had been doing so for years. And maybe, in some strange ways, they had.

She still surprised him. Not with grand gestures, but with the small things: the way she tucked her hair behind her ear when thinking—and how she looked whenever she was about to say something a little too honest. He embraced every one of her quirks, including her habit of saying whatever came to mind—dangerous but adorable. He had the advantage over others in that he never took anything personally or negatively—at least not from her.

It was the subtle activities that impacted him the most—her presence, her pace, her touch, simply the way he felt when he was around her. Nothing had ever compared to that.

The way she looked at him like she didn't want anything somehow made him want to give her everything. When she wanted to be, she was one hundred percent present—something many people struggle with, and something he cherished and simply desired more often.

They found their way to a park, leaves crunching beneath their steps as they wandered a path lined with oaks and fading hydrangeas. They seized the opportunity for another selfie. They had taken several together, but not nearly as many as the number of memories they had created together.

The bench was cold when they sat, but they leaned into each other naturally, their legs brushing together under their layers to keep warm.

"I've been thinking about the poem you sent me," she confessed.

"Yeah?"

"It wasn't just the words," she said, looking straight ahead. "It was how they felt."

He felt quiet. Unsure of what to say but feeling the silence around them, he responded. "I didn't mean to pressure you, just to let you know I was thinking about you, and how."

"No. You haven't pressured me, and I haven't felt that. Actually, I think you're one of the most patient men I've ever met."

He looked at her. Not searching. Not pressing. Just *there*. "So, what have you been thinking about?"

She leaned into him, encouraging his arm to slip around her. "It was just sweet. It made me feel good. I just… think sometimes I feel guilty. This. Us. Whatever *this* is… that we have. I'm just still not sure it's fair to you."

While her words hit him as they had before, again, she may not have been wrong. He wasn't sure of the details in her thoughts, and without asking, the silence extended.

She didn't feel the pressure to break it, ask a follow-up question or ask him for a response. She knew him well. He was either thinking or preparing how to best verbalize what he wanted to say. Her head continued to rest on his shoulder while she waited.

They embraced the silence as he gathered his thoughts. She felt his vibe shift, and with that, so did she. Slightly. Feeling her movement, he decided to push a bit more than he ever expected.

"I know what I want to say, I'm just…"

"Then say it," she interrupted.

"We've known each other for nearly a year. Defined or not, we *have* a relationship, it's just unique. There's nothing wrong with that. Maybe it's why it feels so special. Either way, I have just felt the urge to tell you… I think I love you."

"Wait. What?!"

Her reaction was as quick and unexpected as the words he'd just spoken.

Her body shifted away from his as she turned to face him, more in surprise than discomfort. She hadn't let herself consider what it might feel like to hear those words again. From him. From anyone. Not like this. Not now. Not yet. Maybe ever. And now, here they were. She wasn't sure if she was ready, or if maybe she had been—and was just waiting to hear it. Was she really surprised?

The silence that followed begged to be filled, and quickly. However, neither knew exactly how to break it. He wasn't expecting anything of substance in return, but he also hadn't expected the shock that had obviously come over her.

She realized her reaction hadn't been ideal. She searched his eyes, unsure how to respond.

"I'm sorry. I just wasn't expecting that," she finally confessed.

"Neither was I," he admitted, not sure if he meant his confession, her reaction, or both.

"I'm just not sure how to respond to that."

"I know. I don't feel right apologizing for saying it… it's what I feel… and what I've wanted to say." He continued, trying to relieve some of the pressure she might be feeling. "There are so many ways to interpret that. Just accept it the way that makes you comfortable."

He was right. It could mean several things and be felt in many ways. However, she was pretty sure she knew how he meant it—between them.

"What are you looking for?" she asked gently, readjusting herself back closer to him.

"I'm still figuring that out, but I'd be lying if I said whatever I want didn't include you. I'm in no rush, but eventually, I want a partner. It doesn't have to be the typical relationship society defines. Actually, I would prefer to have something others may not think is possible. What-ever 'we' decide. Someone with whom I want to soak up every ounce of life. You know… *my person*."

She wasn't sure what to say but enjoyed hearing his thoughts. Want-ing to hear him continue, she asked a follow-up question.

"What does *your person* look like?"

"Someone who *wants* me but doesn't *need* me. Maybe in time that *want* becomes a *need*, or just something deeper. Someone that doesn't need to be taken care of… but would let me take care of them… how-ever she wants or however I can. Someone I can trust, with everything, and who inspires and challenges me to never stop with whatever I do. Of course, I want to be the same for them. Too much?"

"No. Not at all. It sounds like something that just doesn't exist. Do you think someone like that is out there?"

"I know she is."

His words landed hard, and she knew she'd walked right into that response. Making an effort to avoid any awkwardness or unwanted pressure, he continued.

"I never thought I would tell someone I loved them again. But I've learned so much and know what I'm looking for, which is a wonderful and terrifying feeling. We can only control half of the equations like this, and I never expected someone like you.

For a long time now, I've felt *you* are my person, and the only thing missing might be that I'm not yours. If that's the case, logic says you can't be mine.

I want your trust… and hopefully, eventually, your heart. But I know that you have to *want* to trust me… and allow that trust to be earned. To give it a chance… to give *me* a chance.

No matter what happens, we can both still get hurt. That's life. No-body can predict tomorrow, but not being able to shouldn't prevent them from living today… and simply manage the future when it comes."

He let the weight of his words sink in and dissolve. He had spoken his mind and now felt the need for a little damage control. Nothing was meant to disrupt anything they had between them, yet he knew the risk he was taking.

"Hey," he said with a light-hearted change of tone trying to bring back the excitement from the heaviness he may have created.

She looked at him with eyes unsure of what to say next.

"I still like you..." he said with a smirk.

She smiled. Larger than he expected. A pleasant surprise.

"... and I don't want anything to change between us," he added.

That encouraged her smile to remain and, at the same time, brought her a sense of peace as she closed her eyes. She lowered her head back to his shoulder.

Feeling awkward about thanking him for his reassurance, she chose a different response.

"I don't want things to change either."

"There's a big difference between thriving and surviving, and I don't want to keep anything from you. I thought it was fair for you to know how I feel and just as unfair for me to keep it inside. Still... no pressure. Right?"

"Right," she responded.

She adjusted herself to kiss him, without hesitation.

It wasn't an easy discussion, but one that might have been needed. If nothing else, to clear the air and maybe reset the stage for whatever was to come.

She kissed him again, doing her best to calm her racing mind. She broke off for a moment to squeeze his hand and look into his eyes. She rested her cheek against his.

"I adore you," she whispered into his ear.

His heart skipped.

"Likewise," he whispered back.

That was good enough.

They worked their way back to the hotel where he was staying. Something a little different that offered her a brief escape as well.

While the conversation had shifted their mood slightly, they each wondered if it had made any impact on their connection.

He opened the door to the room and followed her in. It remained quiet, but anything that could have felt uncomfortable didn't linger for long. Their hands and the small space between them lifted any heaviness that may have existed, as they continued to feel the bond they had always shared.

When he reached out and touched her face, she didn't flinch. Instead, she leaned in, put a hand on his shoulder, and pulled him closer. They both let the silence speak as he kissed her.

It wasn't urgent, not at first. Just the kind of kiss that had been waiting all season. Slow. Certain. The kind that said *finally*. With it, a different kind of passion. She felt it. She felt *him*.

When she kissed him back, it held a bit more intensity. He felt the spark ignite as she took to his shirt and started to unbutton it.

There were no more questions to ask and no more concerns to be addressed.

They were together, again. That was all that mattered. The passion, which had never left, took over again—along with the familiarity and closeness they both longed for.

They undressed each other quickly and without pretense. It was no longer about seduction, but about presence. It was about exploring and leveraging their chemistry. A feeling which neither felt they would find elsewhere.

A new type of trust was emerging. A new understanding and a new type of closeness. A bit more vulnerability. It was about choosing to be in the moment. Completely.

All of it, enhancing what they shared. Together.

They lay tangled in the hush of the room. Arms, legs, breath and heartbeats intertwined.

She quietly rested her head on him, drawing shapes across his chest as he traced idle circles on her back. He felt her hair brush against his face as he took in her scent.

"I'm sorry if I spooked you earlier," he said in an attempt to ensure closure of the topic and that nothing had been damaged between them.

"You should be," she responded in a teasing but reassuring voice while giving him a squeeze. This coaxed a much-needed laugh from him.

"Honestly," she continued, "It was kind of nice to hear. Just unexpected… and I guess… maybe a little scary."

He kissed the top of her head. "Good. But… I didn't mean for it to be scary."

"Oh," she responded quickly. "It wasn't the words that scared me.

I've heard those words a lot in my life… from a lot of different people.

What scared me… is that you meant it.

And that I believe you."

SUMMER

RETURN TO THE CABIN

☀ ☀ ☀

Seasons passed quietly, quickly—like pages turning in a book. The leaves fell, and holidays came and went. Texts, calls, and occasional visits continued—each separated by long pauses. Something still seemed to be missing—unless, of course, they were together. Maybe it was the absence of formality—not something either of them needed, but still…

The irregularity of their time together and the lack of anything substantial often stirred doubts about the future, and sometimes even about the present.

She remained focused on her daughter, on work, on the life she'd built—and continued to build. He worked, wrote, traveled, continued to piece together his future, and longed for more of her.

They never made promises. The effort was sporadic, yet they didn't disappear. Neither of them could.

There were times they nearly drifted apart—moments when the silence stretched too long, too far. Somehow, one of them always reignited the connection. And the thread held. Sometimes, barely. But whenever they were together, they were inseparable. And in those times, it always felt right—as if it were meant to be.

It had been months since they last connected—and truly spoke. And yet, for some reason, the timing now felt right. The past felt far enough away to stop whispering its usual warnings; maybe it wasn't about chasing something new but establishing something real.

While he never fully left, he had been on her mind recently, holding an even stronger presence. She had convinced herself more than once that he wasn't there as often as he was. She hadn't planned to text him—not really. Yet, over the past few weeks, the thought surfaced repeatedly. And every time, she talked herself out of it.

What if he'd moved on?

She told herself it wouldn't matter. As always, she wasn't reaching out for anything serious. Just to say hello. To see how he was. Still, the question lingered—unspoken, but heavy: What if he was no longer *hers* to reach? Either way, they were still friends. Right?

It had been too long. Why did something so simple, so easy, and so good have to feel so difficult? It only seemed that way during spells of absence and longing.

Now, the quiet moments between priorities had increased slightly, and made space for something else. Something more. A thought, a memory—his voice, his companionship, their conversations, the intimacy. That look in his eyes the last time they parted—or any time he looked at her, for that matter. She was still wrestling with whether what they had was a season, a spark, something real or something more.

The text was short and direct.

How are you? You've been on my mind.

His response wasn't nearly as delayed as she thought it might be.

I'm good, thanks. Nice to hear from you. How have you been?

Strange, how a few words on a screen could flood her with emotion. A sense of peace. Just seeing his name light up her phone made her feel more connected. Indeed, it had been too long—again.

I'm good, thank you. Are you interested in catching up?

His reply was simple, familiar, heartfelt.

Always

They scheduled a time to talk, and it didn't take long for it to become a video call. The conversation flowed as easily as ever—no missed beats, full of laughter, questions, and shared moments.

As the topics shifted and a brief pause formed, she took the opportunity.

"So, are you seeing anyone?"

It wasn't quite a confession, but it was something. A door that may have been opening—slowly and tentatively.

There was a pause—maybe wondering why the question hadn't been asked sooner. Maybe debating whether to deflect, since they'd been down this road many times before. Or maybe it was just the weight of the question itself. Regardless, his heart skipped a beat when she asked.

"If I *were*, we probably wouldn't be talking."

"Good answer. Are you?"

"No. I'm not," he confirmed. "You?"

"If I *were*, we probably wouldn't be talking."

He laughed at their colorful, mirrored exchange.

The conversation changed after that—a little deeper, more reflective, more meaningful.

"Would you want to get together again?" she asked.

Then came the pause, which seemed to linger longer than it should. Was it a difficult question, or were there other factors making it so? Had the time come to stay friends, or more likely, acquaintances—formally making a shift and filing their history into just another failed relationship? If so, it was probably long overdue and wouldn't be without merit.

As customary, his heart spoke faster than his brain.

"Yes. Just tell me when."

And just like that, they were planning to see each other again. The conversation continued, nearly three hours, and a plan was eventually made. This time, with a twist. She had an idea. They would meet at the resort where so many of their first memories had taken shape. The cabin. This time, intentionally.

The next day, she called to make a reservation, requesting the same cabin they had shared before—the one where their lives had changed. When she was offered another cabin due to a booking conflict, she quickly convinced herself that it didn't matter. Not really. The reason for being there was what really mattered. That felt good. Secure.

Now, all that was left was waiting.

She arrived late in the morning.

The gravel crunched beneath her tires as the resort emerged from behind a wall of pines—familiar yet different. Summer had softened everything. Where she once remembered the stark silence of snow, wildflowers now framed the path, and pine needles rustled overhead in a quiet hush of green. Birds sang, their calls drifting over the warm breeze like a welcome from an old friend.

She took a slow, steady breath as she gripped the wheel. This place held memories like snowdrifts—beautiful, but dangerous if you stepped wrong.

As she was checking in, the attendant offered a tight, somewhat reluctant smile.

"I'm sorry, ma'am. There was a mix-up, and the cabin you reserved was double-booked. We had to switch your reservation… but we think you'll find this cabin just as nice."

Once again, she reminded herself the location wasn't what mattered. Of course, the irony of being double-booked—and ultimately sharing a room—brought back a memory, and with it a smile to her face.

She stared at the cabin number. A blink. Then another. No—it couldn't be. Her breath gave a strange little kick. The same number. The same cabin. Her first thought was a clerical error. But something about it—something in the way it mirrored the past—felt too perfect.

The attendant was already moving on, handing her the key with a polite nod, unaware he'd just opened a door to more than a room. She didn't argue. She only nodded, barely trusting her voice.

The cabin stood waiting, unchanged—but everything inside her had shifted. Her heartbeat was louder than the footsteps she took across the deck.

Once inside, everything looked untouched, but not unlived. The furniture stood in the same quiet arrangement. The air still held the faint scent of pine and woodsmoke, even in summer. She unpacked slowly, including her clothes and a book she likely wouldn't read. Her movements were quiet, deliberate, and reflective.

She took in the memories, her fingers brushed familiar surfaces— where he had once leaned against the counter, where laughter curled like steam in the cold. It was like walking through a preserved moment. Her chest felt tight. She sat on the edge of the bed, emotions catching up to her. She lay back and closed her eyes.

She woke up slightly confused, her surroundings soft but not unfamiliar. She didn't remember falling asleep, only the wave of memories and emotions when she arrived. The long drive had given her time and space to think—about everything—and time to wonder what the future might hold. What she, or they, might want to create—or not create— or avoid thinking about at all.

She rubbed her eyes and sat up slowly, her thoughts still untangling. It didn't take long to remember where she was—and why it mattered. Then her gaze dropped to the floorboards beneath the bookshelf. A small, recessed panel. She laughed softly. While she would never forget, it had somehow skipped her mind until just now.

She crossed the room, knelt down, and opened the panel with ease.

"Ha! Still got it," she whispered, smiling as her fingers slid the panel open.

She pulled out the familiar contents including the parchment which held *The Snowflake*. Some things were never meant to be taken from this space. But this time, she noticed something else—another envelope— with her name written on the outside.

She knew the handwriting as well as her own heartbeat, which made hers skip with anticipation. She stared at it for a moment before opening it. Instinctively, she flipped to the end first.

My Love—Always.

Her breath caught, and she rose with a rush of emotion, crossing the room to grab one of the wine bottles she'd brought with her.

Now seemed like a good time, and she poured herself a glass, the crisp scent rising to meet her.

She took a sip—cool, bright, and slightly floral—before returning to the bed with both the letter and the glass cradled in her hand. Then, she began to read.

When I'm With You
The most complex of feelings, come from the heart,
To explain them to others is the difficult part.
Yet these feelings I have, always leave me inspired,
And to share them with you, is my only desire.

While I can't list them all, I'll give you a clue—
Of what happens in me, when I'm with you.

It's your beauty I see that captures my stare,
And it starts at the top with the flow of your hair.
Then down to the spark that shines in your eyes—
It catches my heart, and the beats quickly rise.

Of course, there's your smile; nothing as bright,
Lifting my feelings to a breathtaking height.
I can't overlook the soft glow of your skin,
And there's so much to say of your beauty within.

More precious than gold, a vision so rare,
Captivating my eyes, beyond all compare.
Whenever I see you, it seems like the first—
My heart starts to pound, almost ready to burst.

I lose all control and fall for the view,
In everything I see, when I'm with you.

It's your beauty I hear, echoing in my mind,
A sound like no other, and in no other I'd find.
The tone of your voice, the care in your words—
Like angelic music or the sweet song of birds.

Your mind speaks with ambition and grace,
Confidence and drive in each challenge you face.
Positive and happy, curious and playful;
Every moment with you, makes my heart grateful.

All other sounds fade; I know what to do—
You're all that I hear, when I'm with you.

There's nothing I miss when you cross my mind,
Each thought of romance is a treasure to find.
I imagine adventures, laughter, and sun—
Exploring each other as we grow into one.

A lack of discussion is never a threat—
So much more we can learn that we haven't yet met.
Only one thing compares to how much I care,
That's the number of things I want us to share.

These thoughts, old and new, steady and true—
They're all that I think of, when I'm with you.

She paused. The page trembled in her hand—not from cold, but from how her body registered every word. She wasn't sure she was ready to keep reading—but she couldn't stop.

Rising from the bed, she crossed to the window, needing to feel grounded, to remind herself that the world outside still existed.

The light hit the page perfectly.

She blinked through the sudden sting in her eyes and took another sip, grateful for the small comfort in her hand. Leaning her shoulder against the window frame, she continued.

> *It's your beauty I feel, deep in my soul,*
> *A connection that guides me and makes me feel whole.*
> *An energy surge that continues to thrive,*
> *It drives my excitement of being alive.*
>
> *It cannot compare to your passionate kiss,*
> *It carries a spark—one of pure bliss.*
> *What I feel most is that burning desire,*
> *To spend more time with you, which pushes it higher.*
>
> *These sensations endure, persistent and true—*
> *They're all that I feel, when I'm with you.*
> *Perhaps all of this is a fool's point of view,*
> *But I cannot imagine, my life without you.*
>
> *This passion that burns, sometimes fast, sometimes slow,*
> *It's something inside me that continues to grow.*
> *What I see, what I hear, what I think, what I feel—*
> *Each moment with you makes everything real.*
>
> *I have you to thank—and perhaps heaven above,*
> *For showing me this unstoppable love.*
> *I cannot control it, nor would I want to,*
> *This love that consumes me, when I'm with you.*

She stared at the final line, still standing at the window. Her fingers curled tighter around the edges of the paper.

The letter appeared older—but the feelings were not. They pulsed through the room, through her, as if he were there reading it aloud.

"How could you have known?" she whispered into the quiet.

As if the letter had waited for her to return.

She didn't move. Didn't speak.

He hadn't said those words before—not quite—but now, she could hear him in every line. And somehow, she didn't feel quite so alone.

She exhaled slowly as the weight of his words settled warmly over her.

In an age of fast texts and quicker goodbyes, the act of putting love to paper felt almost sacred. Foolish, maybe. But she knew which one it was.

Her gaze dropped again to the poem in her hand. His words expressed everything he couldn't say out loud—each line filled with meaning and hope—meant to melt her heart. Just like a snowflake.

She turned toward the view. The snow was gone—replaced by thick green that stretched as far as the eye could see.

Below, the pool lay still—a crystal-clear oasis nestled behind a stand of trees. Private, quiet, theirs for the weekend. The water shimmered, warmed by several days of sun. It wasn't just the heat that made her feel like she was melting inside.

She closed her eyes and let the quiet settle over her. The wine glass rested in her hand, half-full, while the taste of him still lingered in her thoughts.

She took another long sip—cool, floral, comforting. The afternoon light was golden, bringing a new kind of brightness to everything around her.

It felt like an invitation.

With a quiet breath and a gentle smile, she decided to make her way down to embrace some of the warmth the day still had to offer—seeking sun, stillness, peace—maybe even a little escape.

He wasn't there.

Not yet.

But in her mind, he already was.

Maybe he had always been.

POOLSIDE REVERIE

She still had time to catch some afternoon sunlight—and redirect her thoughts toward the evening ahead.

After dipping her toes in the water, she settled onto a nearby lounge chair. Placing her nearly empty glass of wine beside her, she already felt its warmth spreading through her.

Reclining slightly, she tucked her hair behind her shoulders as a light breeze carried the fresh, green scent of the surrounding trees. The soft rustling of leaves and distant birdsong created a peaceful hush around her. The warmth of the sun seeped into her skin as she breathed deeply, letting her thoughts drift and her body relax.

She began applying sunscreen—an innocent act that soon became something more. It became almost impossible not to imagine his hands assisting her. Fantasies bloomed: his touch, his kiss, his voice whispering her name.

Her body responded before resistance had a chance.

His hands glided over the tops of her feet, massaging the lotion in with a soothing rhythm. She inhaled sharply as she sank deeper into her chair. As his hands slid up the front of her shins, she clenched her teeth to keep from gasping. He moved back down her calves, circling around her knees, each touch strengthening her yearning.

Her eyes remained closed, trusting that the sensation would continue—and, hopefully, progress.

His fingers explored her thighs, still being warmed by the afternoon sun. She shifted slightly, inviting his touch, and he used the opportunity to cover every inch of her legs. One leg drifted open slightly as his fingers grazed the edge of her bikini, briefly slipping beneath before gliding back down her leg. She ached for more of his hands—and the promise of another delicate, deliberate slip beneath the fabric.

This time, his hands slid up the backs of her thighs, again slipping beneath the suit, caressing the lower curve of her ass. She arched her back in response, offering more of herself, encouraging him without words.

His hands moved to her front, and she guided them with her own—placing them on her stomach, inviting more. He massaged her sides and the small of her back, then trailed his fingers up to the strings of her top. Rather than untying them, he left them in place and let his hands move beneath the fabric, brushing the center of her back.

When he finally moved to her front, her heart pounded in her chest. His hands encased her breasts; his fingers brushed her stiffened nipples. She gasped as he pulled her top off, lifting it until it dropped beside her on the deck. His hands cupped her bare breasts, massaging gently, and she overlaid her hands on his, reinforcing the motion—affirming her desire for more.

He moved to her shoulders next, spreading a fresh layer of lotion before trailing his hands down her arms. She lifted them for better access, and his hands continued to her elbows, then her wrists, then her fingers. He laced his with hers, and the simple act of holding hands drew a rush of emotion. It had been too long since they held hands like this, and it stirred something deep inside her.

Raising their joined hands above her head, she felt his body lean closer, his chest brushing against her bare skin. His scent overwhelmed her senses, and she moistened her lips in anticipation. When his lips finally met hers, the kiss was soft, deep, lingering. His tongue gently caressed her lips, sending a wave of pleasure through her limbs, tingling all the way to her toes. The shock of it made her eyes flutter open.

She was alone.

She looked down to see her bikini top lying on the deck beside her. She quickly looked around to confirm it—no one else in sight. Only then did she lift her glass and take the final sip.

The fantasy lingered on her skin like the sun's warmth. She glanced at the pool—cool, crystalline, and impossibly inviting. Perhaps it would help settle her before the late afternoon shadows approached. Leaving her top behind, she dipped her toes in before sliding into the water until it reached her shoulders. After a few moments of floating and cooling off, she hoisted herself onto the edge and let her legs dangle, swirling them slowly.

Her thoughts returned to the moment she had been imagining, which had ended far too quickly. She closed her eyes and let her mind drift again.

She recalled massages from her past and now imagined him behind her. His hands—gentle yet firm. Focused. Easing the tension from her shoulders. She leaned back into his body as he moved her hair aside to press a kiss to the back of her neck, then another, before moving just below her ear. She tilted her head to invite more.

He kissed his way down to her shoulders, and she bent her arms to recline into him a bit more. His arms wrapped around her waist. Her head found his shoulder. When she turned, he was there, waiting, and they kissed again—more urgently. Their mouths, their tongues—nothing was tentative. It was a craving for one another that could not be satisfied.

His hands went back to her stomach, brushing just below her bikini. They met there, then rose to her breasts, which she pressed into his palms with anticipation. He held her tightly, deepening the kiss. She pulled back, panting, sighing, before tipping her head to give him access to her neck once again. His lips and tongue moved in a caressing manner. He continued lower, and she turned back to him, seeking to find his lips with her own.

His hands traveled down, gripping the sides of her bikini bottoms. Two fingers from each hand gently slid underneath the edges of her suit. The smile that broke across her face altered their kissing for a moment—his touch was too much. She shifted her legs apart a little more.

His arms held her steady as his fingers explored deeper under the fabric. She resisted the urge to move despite her body trembling when his fingers found her—warm—wet—waiting—wanting. Her lips parted slightly, her breath hitched. A surge rushed through. Wanting to connect with his eyes, she began to open them. But the sensation of his fingers and his presence instantly started to fade.

No—she didn't want this to end. She quickly closed her eyes and imagined him still with her, but now, he had slipped into the water in front of her.

He approached and placed his hands on her knees. A grateful breath escaped her. His hands slid up the outsides of her thighs, slipping under her suit to caress her ass before returning them to her knees. She opened her legs allowing him to step between them. She placed her arms around his neck, pulling him closer, then kissed him again.

His hands traced her hips while hers cradled his face. They separated slowly, only to let him kiss his way lower—to her chin, her neck, her chest. His fingers gently untied her bottoms and slipped them off. She tilted her hips to help, and they soon joined her bikini top on the deck.

His kissing lingered at her breasts, licking, teasing, biting, tasting. She settled into a new position, feeling the warm deck beneath her center, a sensation of freedom. Placing a hand behind her, he gently helped her recline onto the sun-warmed deck, arms stretched above her, legs still dangling in the water. His hands were now free to explore every inch of her. She arched into his touch, helping him reach beneath her, guiding his hands along her curves.

He slowly backed away, kissing her belly and moving down. One hand traveled down her leg, lifting her foot from the water. He kissed her ankle, her calf, her thigh. His other hand rested near her neck. She guided and coaxed it to her lips, drawing his fingers in as her tongue began its sensual dance.

He was at her center—she felt him there.

He spread her legs a bit more. Gently. Reverently. Two fingers traced the warm, slick path at her entrance to her clit and back again. Slow, then a bit faster, then slowly again. Changing focus, he watched her every reaction. Every sigh, every arch, every tremble. Keeping her guessing but focused wherever she indicated pleasure. Her responses. Her desires. Her body provided him all the guidance he needed, which was just as pleasurable to him.

He leaned in to taste her—soft, reverent kisses at first, then deeper, more focused strokes. His tongue moved with purpose, alternating between broad sweeps and precise circles. His hands moved beneath her ass to provide comfort and hold her. It felt like he was painting a masterpiece, her body his canvas.

She could tell—he wanted more. So did she.

When he drew her clit into his mouth and began to suck, her world tilted. Releasing it, he returned to the stroking with his tongue. He remained steady, patient and consistent. He followed her signals and continued, finding the perfect spot, with the perfect pressure and the perfect rhythm. Her breath became shallow as she trembled. She gasped, writhed, tried to hold still.

"Stay… right… there…" she whispered between ragged breaths.

Her muscles tightened. Unable to fight the urge, her legs rose and wrapped around him, pulling him closer. He moaned into her, the vibration pulling her toward the edge. She clutched his hair, overwhelmed by pleasure, completely undone, surrendering completely.

The feeling was consuming, euphoric, complete. Her body pulsed against his mouth. He slowed, letting his lips rest gently against her. Light, gentle kisses. Her fingers tangled in his hair—not to guide, just to touch. The sensation of him between her legs was comforting, and a warm peaceful feeling of trust spread over her. A soft laugh erupted. He heard it, and the joy it carried settled into him, knowing he had the pleasure of helping her feel this amazing.

After a few relaxing breaths, she stretched her arms above her head. The sun had slipped behind the trees, and cool shadows began to gather at the edge of her reach.

She hesitated to open her eyes, not wanting the fantasy to end.

When she did, she saw the fading warmth of the sun now mingling with the cool shadows creeping across the pool. The water glistened, still kissed by sunlight, and remained empty. The vividness of the fantasy lingered in her skin—his touch, the whispered sounds, the tender kisses—but reality gently returned, wrapping around her like a familiar embrace.

Her breath slowed, and with it, clarity.

There was something undeniable between them—an electric pull beneath their attraction, friendship, and desire. A connection that had always been there, waiting. Not just chemistry, but something fierce, fragile, and real. And as much as she had tried to guard her heart, she could no longer deny the truth settling quietly within her.

Maybe it was time.

Time to stop holding back or at least be more open to explore the potential. Time to step past fear and hesitation and give love a chance— not for perfection, not for certainty, but for the possibility of something real, something worth trying. To take a risk. To make an effort.

She sighed, a slow smile tracing her lips as she rose from the pool's edge—lighter now, like a weight had been released.

Time for one final dip before the shadows claimed the day.

The water wrapped around her—cool, calm, forgiving. She let it hold her body—her heart, and her still-lingering desire.

The warmth of the wine was fading, leaving space for something new—a fragile but unmistakable realization.

If she was ever going to trust anyone again, it would be *him*.

The thought both unsettled her and settled her heart.

No longer just a longing—

but a silent admission.

A tentative hope she hadn't dared to feel before.

THE QUIET BETWEEN

☀ ☀ ☀

The early evening cast long shadows across the cabin floor. She convinced herself to relax with a book to pass the time. She could shower, but she didn't want to risk missing him when he arrived. It could wait.

She paced restlessly from the window to the fireplace, then finally sank into the cushions of the couch. She read the same paragraph three times before sighing and snapping the book shut. Even the opportunity to get a little work done didn't offer its usual comfort.

She wasn't fooling herself.

Her gaze moved to the fireplace as she was flooded with more memories—his voice, low beside her; the brush of his fingertips; the careful way they'd circled each other—everything.

Some memories she let rise, embracing the feeling, while others she would simply let melt away.

A smile tugged at her lips as she considered the possibilities—the potential that had yet to be explored or even named. She stood, her smile shifting into a nervous grin. She bit her lip and wondered what to do next. There was a possibility again. A chance, however fragile, for something neither of them had dared believe in before.

She walked to the window. The sky had deepened to navy, and the first stars would soon be piercing through the canopy. Her reflection stared back at her from the glass, and for a moment, she didn't look away.

With the cool night air approaching, she decided to start a small fire. As it slowly began to burn, she moved back to the window and stood quietly, watching the shimmer of the pool reflect across the windowpane. The hush in her chest wasn't anxiety but anticipation. Excitement. Something sincere.

His headlights swept through the cabin, momentarily flooding it with light.

She flinched, then stilled.

She didn't know what this visit would bring. Closure. Clarity. Or something else entirely. But she knew she wasn't ready to let go.

The knock at the door was soft—*just once*. She opened it before a second could land.

He stood there, hair tousled from the drive, his smile uncertain, but his eyes steady. For a moment, they just looked at each other. She was about to step forward when he stepped in to meet her.

The embrace wasn't rushed, but lasting and strong—the kind you don't want to end.

Neither of them spoke. It wasn't needed because the silence felt familiar. It was comfortable. Safe. They stood there, holding on, and for a while, that was enough.

He finally broke the silence as they separated slightly, still holding hands.

"Nice place you've got here," he said with his eyes still on her.

She narrowed her gaze playfully. "You're not going to believe this…"

He didn't blink. Just waited. A smile trying not to form, which was nearly impossible.

"Wait. Did you make this happen?"

The corners of his mouth finally lifted fully. "Remember our snow-cat chauffeur?"

"Not sure I'll ever forget him."

"Well… he remembered us too and agreed. We had to stay here. It's all about relationships."

She laughed softly, shaking her head as she pulled him into another embrace. Her voice softened.

"I'm really glad we're here."

"Likewise."

They held each other a bit longer, soaking in the overdue feeling.

"I've missed you," he whispered.

She pulled back just enough to look at him.

"I've missed you too," she said.

She thought about mentioning the poem but decided to wait—it might bring up something too heavy, too soon. For now, this was perfect. It was a reunion that should never have waited this long.

Her renewed energy finally came out. "Get in here! Do you need anything?"

"A shower. Maybe a bite to eat," he suggested.

"Perfect. You shower first—then it's my turn."

"Deal. Are you hungry? I picked up dinner."

"Yes! I haven't eaten all day—let's eat first!"

They talked like best friends who never ran out of things to say. They talked about work, the drive, the cabin, and how summer had changed the look of everything around them.

And when they weren't talking, the silence was just as comforting.

Their hands continued to find each other, as always, and even when they weren't touching, they stayed close.

No pressure. No challenging questions. Just the two of them. Present.

After dinner, she sat quietly for a moment, then reached for her journal. Her fingers brushed against the folded page. Now it felt right.

"I found something earlier," she said.

He looked up. "What kind of something?"

She held out the envelope with her name on it. "Guess where I found this."

Recognition flickered in his eyes. "I think I might know."

"I figured you would."

He smiled. More in memory than surprise. "I wondered if you'd find it."

"I was shocked," she admitted. "I read it once… *then again.*"

"I'm glad you found it. I'm surprised you looked, but not really."

"You wrote that for *me?*"

"Well, I did write it. *About* you for sure. But I guess I did write it *for* you as well. I was passing through the area a few months ago and wasn't really sure what I was doing at the time. I think I just wanted to feel closer to you… so I stayed over a night. I guess I felt the need to leave something behind. Something that felt like… me. Or maybe… us."

"You did," she said, moving closer. She settled onto his lap, her hand on his chest. "It meant something… it still does."

He exhaled slowly. "I didn't want to push you. But I also couldn't just disappear. Or not be me."

"I'm glad you didn't push," she said, her gaze searching for his. "Really glad. But I'm here now. We both are."

She leaned in, wrapped her arms around him, pulled him close, and whispered into his ear. "Thank you," her lips brushing against his ear, "for waiting."

This landed hard. For both of them. The words settled between them. Weightless, and yet, everything.

He let out a slow breath against her neck, unsure exactly what she meant—but it was clearly something good. Letting himself lean into the moment, he decided to build on her words.

"I don't let people in, yet you found your way," he whispered back.

She pulled away just enough to meet his eyes. "I didn't mean to."

"No? Well, that doesn't matter. You did… and now you're there to stay, for better or worse."

She smiled and rested her forehead against his.
"For better," she whispered.
And just like that, everything else faded.
They didn't need to say more. The quiet said it all.
They had the rest of the evening to let unfold—together.

TRUSTING TOUCH

The small fire had faded to a soft orange glow, and the cabin had grown quiet except for the occasional creak of cooling wood. She was still curled in his lap, cheek against his shoulder, his hand tracing slow, absent-minded circles along her back. They savored the moment for as long as the silence would allow.

Eventually, she leaned back to look at him, her lips brushing into a smile.

"You mentioned wanting a shower," she said with a teasing smile.

He chuckled, his voice low. "Definitely. Is that a hint?"

She kissed his cheek and laughed.

"No." She slipped out of his arms. "You go. I'll take mine after."

By the time he returned, hair damp and a towel tied around his waist, she had tidied the space and dimmed the lights. Her robe hung loosely around her waist as she moved through the room in soft silence.

"Your turn," he said gently, brushing her arm as they passed each other.

She looked over her shoulder. "Ten minutes. Then I'm all yours."

His smile was eager as he called softly.

"Are you back yet?"

Her skin was warm and flushed after stepping out of the shower, and she noticed how relaxed she'd become as she began to dry herself. Wrapping herself in a large towel, she made her way into the bedroom.

The lights were off, but she could see easily enough from the moonlight and the candles, which had been strategically placed around the room.

The pleasant aroma captured her attention, as did the fresh towels spread across the bed—inviting her to lie down on them.

She knew what he had in mind and slipped off her towel, lay down on her stomach, and draped it back over her to keep warm.

Closing her eyes, she began to lose herself in the soft music playing in the background. Falling into a state of relaxation, she felt his touch on her shoulder, sending a slight chill down the side of her body.

He moved his hands from her shoulders down her back to her legs, pausing at her feet. Her anticipation grew as she heard the sound of oil being worked over his hands and through his fingers.

The first touch was gentle, yet firm on her feet. Starting at her toes, he worked slowly on each one before moving down her arches to her heels.

To her surprise, the way his fingers swirled around didn't tickle. He moved from her heels to her ankles, then slowly back to her toes.

He continued his work by caressing her tendons. Once the oil and warmth of his touch penetrated her feet, the strength of his fingers slowly worked their way up the muscles of her calves.

His hands moved fluidly, tracing her curves up to the backs of her knees, slipping beneath her legs to smooth the front of her thighs.

Each stroke was warm and deliberate. As he paused for more oil, she sensed the warm tingling sensation on, and between her legs.

His warm touch quickly returned to the back of her thighs, just below the towel covering her backside. The long, smooth strokes moved slowly up and down the backs of her legs.

Continuing down the outsides, his fingers pulsated in turn as they made their way to her inner thighs and slowly out again. He kept the rhythm varied, teasing her with each pass. Each time his fingers moved closer to the towel.

Any lingering tension in her legs melted away as his hands and fingers moved closer and closer to the aching warmth and slickness building between her thighs.

As the pleasure continued, he worked back down her legs, slowly and firmly, before cradling her feet in his hands once again.

Even more relaxed, her mind loosened its grip. She let go—of restraint, of control—fully surrendering to the care of his intimacy.

Slowly, his fingers crossed the towel covering her legs, over her ass, up the small of her back and finally to her shoulders.

His thumbs traced slow circles along her neck, as if trying to locate any tension and melt it away—each pass a silent promise.

His fingers gently followed along, providing a sensual, tickling feeling to accompany the pressure of his thumbs, which helped soften any lingering tension.

She felt him lean down into her. His breath. His lips. His tongue. All danced along her neck, sending goosebumps trailing down her spine.

Reverent and slow, it ignited more than just her senses. His lips moved away and quickly returned, lower this time. She felt them part slightly, his tongue tasting her soft skin at the base of her neck.

He adjusted the towel to ensure it revealed her entire back, resting just above the beautiful curves of her backside.

His hands began low, just above the towel, and slowly moved up her spine. She felt his strength easing any remaining tension from her body.

When they reached her shoulders, he let them slide down each arm—alternating the squeezing of his fingers all the way to her hands.

He let them intertwine with hers as he held her hands for a moment while he returned to her neck to place a few kisses and take in her scent.

His hands released hers as he moved back to her shoulders where he spent a little more time focusing.

He moved slowly down her sides, returning up the middle of her back and down again to the towel still resting peacefully on her curves.

During his movements, she felt his fingers slip beneath the towel. With each pass, his hands explored a little deeper, more boldly until he was caressing her entire backside.

The towel no longer covered much. Concentrating his movements on her lower back and backside, each time he got close to her wetness, she lifted her hips slightly, hoping his hands would find their way closer to the bed and underneath her.

He moved them over her hips, stopping there, which presented a certain amount of pleasure and torture.

The next time his hands swept to her backside, one finger dipped lower, between her cheeks, tracing a forbidden path that made her breath hitch.

Her legs parted slightly to provide him with the freedom to work, and as an invitation to explore.

He felt how wet she was and decided to remove the towel completely.

Though she wanted to reciprocate, pleasure held her still, letting him continue his magic.

Her breath caught as another finger traced even lower than before. Her muscles tightened in response.

His hands glided over her entire body once again. From her feet to her calves, pausing at her thighs.

Sweeping across her back to her shoulders and neck, back down her arms, taking her hands in his.

Holding them still. Fingers connected.

She felt his breath on her ear as he whispered.

"May I see you?"

She turned over slowly, the candlelit air brushing her bare skin like approval.

Despite her vulnerability, a sense of calm settled over her. Eyes closed, she focused on what pleasure might come next.

Expecting his hands, she was surprised when instead she felt a soft kiss on the top of her foot—followed by a second on the other.

His hands followed quickly, taking her feet into his hands and moving up to her knees.

Spending only a moment before moving to her thighs—she felt a slight chill the closer he got between her legs.

He explored with increasing boldness, each touch drawing nearer to where she ached for his touch.

His hands slid up her body as he let a couple of fingers and his thumb gently glide over the spot still waiting for his attention.

His hands wandered over her hips a few times before returning to her thighs—brushing fingers against her increasing wetness.

He was ready to explore more as he let his hands move to her stomach.

A surge passed through her as his breath warmed her thighs—then came his lips.

Realizing his mouth was so close to tasting her, she moved her hips slightly.

Lifting her backside off the bed, she wanted his tongue to find its way to her.

When she realized he had moved on, the torture continued. Her hips returned to their relaxed position.

But his hands had already found her breasts, and his lips were finding their way up her stomach, leaving a trail of kisses along the way.

His touch on her breasts was wonderful, his hands occasionally shifting focus to her nipples as they peaked in response to his touch.

He moved to the front of her shoulders, spending time caressing before trailing down her arms once again.

As his hands reached hers, they clenched together. Anticipating another kiss, she instead felt his soft, wet tongue as it gently traced a path between her breasts, sending another chill from his mouth to her toes.

He slid to one breast and drew her nipple into his mouth, savoring the soft gasp it pulled from her.

When their hands released, he moved to the other breast, giving it equal attention.

Moving away, his hands settled on her hips. She opened her eyes slightly, catching his gaze full of desire.

Time seemed to pause—only the sound of their breathing filled the room, their heartbeats in total sync.

Their connection was in place.

A slow smile spread across his face as he saw her completely relaxed and trusting in the pleasure he was providing. This eased her even more.

Her hands cupped his face, drawing him to her for a kiss which seemed like it was years in the making. She whispered against his lips, "I've *missed* this. I've missed *you*."

It started slow, but their passion quickly deepened as their tongues met and danced.

Not quite finished with the massage, he let her rest her head on the bed and began trailing kisses down her body.

Pausing at her navel, he kissed it gently, then slid his hands up her legs, encouraging them to part for him.

His tongue continued downward, seeking the sweet taste they had both been craving.

She felt his breath between her thighs, his hands holding and caressing her.

He continued kissing, inching closer until his tongue finally met her wetness.

The sensation was incredible for both.

She welcomed the increasing pleasure as his tongue slowly made love to her.

Her hands tangled in his hair, silently urging him on as waves of pleasure rippled through her.

She bent her knees, and his hands gripped the tops of her legs, pulling himself closer.

Unable to contain herself, she sat up and quickly removed the towel wrapped around him, revealing his erection, which had been aching for attention since he first touched her.

Their bodies pressed close, still glistening with oil, the warmth intoxicating.

Her breasts pressed to his chest; his erection nestled firmly against her thigh.

He leaned in, showering her neck with kisses, shifting side to side as his hands gripped her ass, pulling her tightly against him.

When she lifted her head, their eyes met, halting everything.

They smiled and shared a laugh, a silent, powerful connection passing between them.

Along with the intimacy, trust, passion and ecstasy—both of them felt safe.

Their smiles faded as their faces drew near.

Their hands embraced; their lips touched—long, soft, and genuine—as they gazed deeply into each other's eyes.

The love they felt was raw and real, more profound than ever before.

Their lips parted as the kissing intensified.

She moved to her back, pulling him on top of her.

Legs wrapped around him, arms clasped tightly.

Their kissing paused briefly, eyes locked in mutual adoration, seeing deeply into each other.

They held each other as closely as they could.

He pushed forward, sliding deep inside her.

Their breaths hitched in unison, fueling a fresh surge of pleasure.

She used her legs to pull him closer as he thrust harder and deeper.

Lifting himself slightly, he looked down at her, desire blazing anew.

She raised her hips for deeper penetration.

Their eyes locked again, pushing them to the brink.

She saw the passion in his face, the tenderness in his eyes, and something unspoken passed between them.

The way she looked at him undid him completely.

He moved with fierce passion, their pleasure built to a level never experienced.

Their bodies moved together in a rhythm born of love and longing, each thrust an answer to a question they hadn't dared ask.

Breathing grew rapid, moans louder; grips tighter as they both rode the crescendo of pleasure as it rolled over their bodies together.

As the intensity faded, he lowered himself onto her, breath still short, kissing still passionate.

After a few moments, he rolled to his side.

She curled up against him, half atop his chest.

They sighed, exhausted yet fulfilled.

Both struggled to find the appropriate words.

However, as always, no words were needed.

A smile, a shared glance, hands touching, noses brushing, soft lips meeting, foreheads pressed together.

These small but powerful actions spoke more to the love between them than any words ever could.

Around them, candlelight flickered, gently casting soft shadows across their skin.

Two bodies—now one story—written in touch.

Told in silence, in something they felt they may have finally found.

WORTH WAITING FOR

Their time at the cabin was now filled with even more memories—from that first unexpected visit to everything that had unfolded since. But now, something new lingered beneath the surface—not quite spoken, not quite hidden.

A quiet shift. A hint of what might come next.

It wasn't uncomfortable—just present. Just waiting.

As always, their time together felt effortless, comforting. But again, it slipped away too quickly. That familiar sense of looming separation was drawing near.

As he zipped the last compartment of his bag, a familiar ache settled in his chest. He looked around and, not seeing her, walked to the window.

She was outside, sitting alone by the pool.

He made his way down the steps and crossed the path steadily.

"Hey, beautiful," he said softly, testing a bit of confidence.

"You really mean that, don't you? Beautiful," she asked, skipping the small talk.

He didn't hesitate—meeting her where she was, wherever the conversation needed to go.

"Yes, I do. Inside and out. With all my heart."

"I get the feeling you're not going to change your mind." Her voice cracked slightly. "And you're likely not giving up on me. Not going away... are you?"

It seemed she might have finally accepted his feelings were as real as he had indicated.

"No. Not a chance. Not unless you force me to in some way." He tried to lighten the mood, if needed. "Take that as either a blessing or a curse."

"I've been doing some thinking these past several months."

He sat down beside her without saying a word, giving her the space she might need. He knew her comment could lead them down any number of paths—or all of them at once. Regardless, he was all in for whatever was coming.

"I'm not sure I'll ever be looking for a relationship," she said.

His heart ached. He wasn't sure what hurt more—her words or how deeply he understood them—and maybe even expected them. A lump rose in his throat. He said nothing. Just stayed with her—listening, patient.

"You said you weren't seeing anyone."

He remained focused. The way he nodded was quiet confirmation—the answer she'd been hoping for.

"I know we've kept in touch… not much… probably not enough… and we've never had expectations. Have you dated anyone else?" she asked, unsure what to expect and unsure what she wanted to hear.

"I've gone out a few times," he said without missing a beat. The honesty in his voice pulled her back into the moment. She looked at him, surprised by his honesty. He smiled in return, recognizing the quiet weight behind her question.

"And?"

"As cliché as it sounds… none of them were *you*. You set the bar pretty high. Honestly, I think *we* set the bar pretty high." She smiled in silent agreement.

"What about you?" he asked.

"I tried a few times," she admitted.

"And?" he returned with the same powerful question.

"I think I was trying to find you… in someone else. And I kept realizing that wasn't going to happen. I also kept recalling how I don't want a relationship. And if I did, I knew what it should feel like… or at least how I wanted it to feel. And that always brought me back to you."

His heart warmed. He wasn't sure what to say, so he tried to support her while keeping his biased thoughts as neutral as possible.

"It's a challenge… nearly impossible… to find someone you're attracted to, have a friendship with, and to share unexplainable chemistry. On top of that, having the timing be right for both is a minor miracle."

She held his gaze. Was he really this romantic? Charmingly oblivious? Maybe both. One thing was certain. While they had never spent consistent time together—and what time they did share was sporadic, his actions never wavered from who he was and how he made her feel.

They'd never raised their voices, and while there were awkward moments, they always resolved them gently—with care for the other.

"I still think this is unfair to you," she said quietly. "I can't promise you anything, and I really don't *want* to promise you, me, or anyone else… anything. I don't want that pressure."

"I don't want that either, but I do know I want you in my life. If I have to accept you as a friend to maintain our connection, so be it. I'll do that as long as I can. I may always want more, but I'll try not to push. If something pulls me away or you decide I'm not the one for you... then I guess it wasn't meant to be. I'll treasure what we've had… without any regrets.

I don't want to think about the future. We can't predict anything. I just want to focus on now… and let the future unfold. And I'd rather do that together."

"That sounds nice, it just seems like that's been our story." She sighed and moved closer to him. "I don't feel I'm 'the one' for anyone, and it's weird to feel that I'm okay with that. It's also human nature for people to get bored and move onto whatever, or whoever, is next. It seems like they don't even need a reason anymore."

He laughed.

She looked at him, curious as to what made him laugh.

"Since my divorce, I've been paying more attention and think I've found six things that usually end a relationship. I'm sure there are more, but for me, it's been limited to those six."

Her mood lifted a little. She raised her brow in quiet curiosity—inviting more without needing to ask. He chuckled again.

"Okay," he said, gathering his thoughts.

"The first is when someone is too desperate. Someone who wants an all-out relationship right away and moves too quickly.

The second is when someone is just way too busy to date, which is fine, then just don't date. Or, be honest about things because you never know what might be acceptable, or even possible.

Another reason is when someone wants to date, but only on *their* terms. They only make an effort when it's convenient for them and usually leave the other person to do most of the work."

She held up her hand, to interrupt.

"Okay, can I jump in? This is fascinating but do any of these apply to us, or me?"

"Well," he replied with a laugh, "the first doesn't apply to either one of us, obviously."

The look on her face revealed she was still awaiting a response.

"No," he added more seriously. "You've always been open and honest about what you want… and what you don't want. And when it comes to effort, we've always known we're in different stages of life. Your responsibilities haven't allowed the same flexibility as mine, and I've accepted that. It's been my choice.

I've just always hoped that someday things might shift to allow for a change. That's life. And if that happened, we would adapt as well. I hope that makes sense."

"It does," she replied, "and I appreciate you acknowledging that. Even if I don't want a relationship, I've always given what I could, given our situation."

"You have," he agreed. "Maybe not ideal. But you've always been present. And—here we are."

"Okay… three more reasons? Let's hear them."

"There are those that only want physical intimacy. I used to think that was just a guy thing. Turns out… it's not."

"Okay—" she said with a laugh. "Is that either of us?"

He laughed as well.

"No. Well… maybe to some degree it's both of us… then that's okay!" He winked. "I'm kidding. I think we share something far beyond *only* physical intimacy, which is what makes 'that part of us' so amazing. Just my opinion."

"I agree with that. The other two?"

"Serial daters," he continued. "They go out a few times, get spoiled, maybe share a little intimacy, and then move on. Sometimes they disappear, even if things seem great and have real potential. They linger just enough to keep you guessing, but either way, it's a game."

"And the last reason?"

"Those who still need to heal. We're all broken in our own ways, and if someone hasn't had the time or made the effort to figure things out, it's hard to meet them in a safe space. They'll never be happy with someone unless they find happiness on their own.

You can't hold that against someone because everyone heals in different ways and in their own time. It just means they're not a good fit… right now... which takes us back to the topic of timing. It needs to be the right time for both."

She let it all settle as he recharged from his sharing. He had clearly thought a lot about these things—and seemed confident in what his experiences had taught him about himself and what he truly wanted.

He knew what he was seeking, and why. She looked at him with a new kind of curiosity.

"You should write a book." She laughed.

He chuckled. "I should."

He took her hand. It had been a good conversation, but he still wasn't sure where it was leading. He waited, letting her guide things toward whatever had been on her mind from the beginning. There was no rush. Eventually, she spoke again.

"I'm not sure what the future holds… or where I fit into your life," she said. Her eyes searched for his, hoping he might help fill the silence.

"I believe people come into our lives for a moment, for a lesson, or for a lifetime," he said gently. "The heartache only happens when you put them in the wrong category."

She looked at him carefully, wanting to ask but hesitating. Then, slowly, she gave in.

"Which category do you think I'm in?"

He reached over, taking both of her hands in his.

"We're way beyond a moment. And I've learned a lot from you… and about myself, because of you. So yeah, plenty of lessons."

She didn't look away, waiting for more.

"Honestly, I don't know. And maybe I won't until years from now, looking back, with or without you in my life. But until then… I'd love for you to keep asking me that question. Every day… for the next fifty years… give or take."

She paused. Looking at him. Putting aside any instinct that she might normally have felt. Her fingers pressed gently into his—a quiet signal he understood instantly.

"Do you still think I'm someone worth waiting for?" she asked.

"Always."

"You must really think I'm something," she said.

He smiled softly. "Not something. Everything."

Her breath caught. Then—"My poet." It was the only thing that came to mind.

His eyes stayed warm and steady. After everything they'd just shared, he still wanted her in his life, no matter what shape it might take—short term or long.

She could see the quiet battle in him—the effort to hold back tears, unsure where this conversation was going to land.

Maybe it was time. Maybe it wasn't.

Maybe he deserved a chance. Maybe she did too.

Maybe they both did, together.

"I'd like to see you again after today. Sooner rather than later," she said, a smile tugging at her lips. "If you're still up for that."

He smiled back, relief quietly written across his face.

"I can't promise I won't mess it up," she said, "but I think I'd like to give us a try."

"That's all either of us can do."

"So... no promises, then. Just honesty. No pressure. No expectations. Deal?"

"Deal."

She hesitated, then let out a soft laugh.

"Well then... maybe we could think about something a little more formal. I don't know if 'boyfriend' quite fits... but maybe we can think of something."

He blinked—surprised—and smiled. He hadn't expected that.

He studied her face—as if memorizing it again.

Neither of them said anything—both holding their breath.

Her gaze lingered—steady and warm. Her smile told him what she was waiting to hear—perhaps even what she was expecting him to say.

He smiled back, eyes locked on hers and gave in.

"I love you," he whispered.

"Come here, you!" she said, pulling him quickly into her arms. She held him as tightly as she could.

"I think I love you, too," she whispered, as if it had been waiting on her lips for a very long time.

They held each other for several moments, wrapped in a comfort they felt could never be matched.

Eventually, they pulled back—just enough for their eyes to meet. Then came the inevitable kiss.

It may have been their most vulnerable kiss yet—perhaps their strongest—but certainly their most intimate.

One season of their story had concluded.

They didn't know exactly what would come next.

But something had taken root.

And for now, that was enough.

A new season—quiet, certain, and finally ready—had begun.

EPILOGUE

Several quiet seasons had passed. It was spring again.

No sudden declarations, no dramatic changes. Just small things, in the months following their return to the cabin. And somehow, in all that quiet, something was taking shape.

They stayed in touch more regularly, more intentionally, with virtual date nights whenever possible. Touchpoints came more frequently—sometimes long, sometimes just a quick goodnight. But it was something. A comfort.

They managed regular visits, a few nights a month when schedules allowed. It wasn't always easy, but it worked. They were finding their way, learning more about one another—what worked and what didn't. *That was the point.*

In time, he relocated closer to her. The freedom to work from anywhere gave him options, yes—but this time, it was for her—for them. Proximity wasn't about convenience. It was about being present. About allowing the potential to be explored, regardless of the outcome.

The move wasn't really about geography. It was about showing up.

He still divided time with his daughters, whose lives were entering new phases—more independent, less centered around him.

They kept separate places, preserving freedom and flexibility, without worry if plans changed. Trust grew, along with their understanding of each other. Living nearby took some getting used to, but they navigated it well—no expectations, no need to define anything.

They were simply—together.

Not formal, not informal—just understood.

One afternoon, his phone buzzed with a message:

Want to meet for dinner?

He responded quickly:

Absolutely! Can't wait!

She arrived at the restaurant to find him already waiting at a table. The gentle hum of quiet conversation filled the air like a warm blanket as the waitress greeted her with a bright smile.

He stood to greet her and took her hand as she sat beside him. Leaning over, he gave her a soft kiss on the cheek.

"Hi, beautiful," he said with a smile.

She didn't answer at first—just met his gaze with her own quiet smile.

"How was your day?"

"Good," she said. "Had a few things to get done. Kind of a busy morning, but an easier afternoon."

The familiar waitress approached their table.

"It's lovely to see you two here again," she said. "You're kind of one of my favorite stories. Cutest couple ever. I'll be back shortly."

"She still thinks we're a couple," she said.

He didn't comment—just continued to watch her as she reached and took his hand.

"Maybe that's not such a bad idea," she said softly. "I think I might like that."

He smiled. "Well, I think I still like you."

Her gaze held his. A beat passed, quiet and sure.

"Well," she said, her voice almost a whisper, "I'm pretty sure I love you."

The poet in him had no words—only the quiet bloom of something taking root beneath the surface.

The timing felt right. He reached into his pocket and pulled out a small, polished key, placing it gently on the table in front of her.

She looked at him with a smile, one brow raised.

"For my place," he said softly, eyes meeting hers. "No pressure. Just if you ever want to drop by. It's not a promise or a demand… just a simple way to say you're welcome. Anytime."

Her breath caught as she slipped the key quickly into her pocket and squeezed his hand a little tighter. The warmth between them lingered like a quiet promise.

"Thank you," she said with a smile that continued to grow.

His phone buzzed early one morning. He picked it up to read her message.

Are you available to meet in the park around noon?

He responded.

Of course! I'll be there!

He arrived to find her sitting on a familiar bench. She reached up to take his hand as he sat beside her. He leaned over and gave her a kiss.

"Hi, handsome," she said as her eyes met his.

"Hi, How are you?"

"Good," she said. "Busy day, but maybe we can get together tomorrow night."

"I'd like that," he said. "I was surprised to get your message. I thought you had mom duty this morning."

"Yeah, about that…" she began.

"Mom!" a voice called from a distance.

She turned to see her daughter running toward them—barefoot in the grass, ponytail bouncing, arms outstretched, like the world belonged to her. Bright. Alive. Unfiltered joy.

This wasn't just about today.

It was about trust—about opening a door that had been closed for a long time.

She turned to him—nervous, maybe, but sure.

"Would you like to meet my daughter?"

He hadn't asked for this—had never dared to expect it.

And yet, here she was, inviting him into the part of her life that mattered most. A gentle stirring of something new growing beneath the surface.

He was speechless.

They still didn't know exactly what they were building—if anything.

But it was real.

And real was enough.

Whatever it turned out to be—they would build it together.

Not all stories need a grand display,

Some grow quietly, day by day.
No promises made, no ties that bind—
Just trusting hearts and space to find.

A NOTE FROM JASON

Thank you for spending time with *Seasons of Intimacy*.

If you've made it this far—I'm truly honored. This book reflects the intimacy, timing, and emotional honesty I value deeply—and continue to seek—as I hope you will as well.

If any moments touched you or left a lasting impression, I'd love to hear from you. Stories are most powerful when they're shared—and hearing how this one may have spoken to you would mean the world. Feel free to reach out anytime at jasonschubertauthor@gmail.com.

If you enjoyed the book, please consider leaving a review on Amazon. Your feedback means a great deal—helps others discover the story and keeps writers like me inspired to keep going.

I hope to share more stories or publications in the future. If all goes well, I hope we find our way back to each other when that time comes.

Thank you again, truly, for reading.

With sincere thanks and gratitude,

Jason

ACKNOWLEDGMENTS

The first people I want to thank are, ironically, the two who *shouldn't* be reading this—my daughters. At least, not until they're older.

While certain elements of this book are intended for mature readers, my deeper hope is that the heart of it shines through—a story of attraction, friendship, chemistry and trust—truly a *love* worth waiting for. My wish is that they, too, one day find a connection as meaningful and enduring as the one shared by these characters.

To those who believed in me—thank you. Not just for supporting this book, but for encouraging me in so many parts of my life, often when I needed it most.

To those whose guidance and support helped bring this book to life. While I knew writing would be a challenge; I had no idea how winding the road would be even after the final page was written.

Lastly, though it may seem unusual, I want to thank those who have played a part in my life when it comes to *matters of the heart*. To those who never gave my heart a chance, or who broke it. To those I let slip away, or whose hearts I may have broken in return. I believe everything happens for a reason, and that each experience brings something worth learning. While some of these storylines have concluded, perhaps a few of them still have chapters to be written—in this life or the next.

E.M.

ABOUT THE AUTHOR

Jason Schubert grew up two hours west of Chicago in *Pecatonica, Illinois*, and has long been fascinated by the stories people carry—both spoken and unspoken. He earned a bachelor's degree in human resource management with a minor in psychology from *Northern Illinois University*. Much of his career has been dedicated to leadership and talent development around the world.

Jason has worked with national and international organizations, using his expertise and certifications to help individuals and teams grow both personally and professionally. He has designed, led, and facilitated leadership programs and workshops for global audiences, and continues this work through his consulting.

Alongside his career, Jason has nurtured a lifelong passion for writing. In 2025, he began transforming his love of storytelling into a larger creative pursuit. With additional projects in development, *Seasons of Intimacy* is his debut novel.

To learn more about Jason, visit www.jasonschubertauthor.com.